G000079620

THE VULCAN WHO GOT INTO PRINT

BY THE SAME AUTHOR...

Animals Tame and Wild (with his father, the late Gilbert Phelps)
Agent from Hell
Underbelly of Cambridge
Keeping It Short
A World Ruled by Mice

THE VULCAN WHO GOT INTO PRINT

John Phelps

Matador
Unit E2 Airfield Business Park,
Harrison Road, Market Harborough,
Leicestershire. LE16 7UL
Tel: 0116 2792299
Email: books@troubador.co.uk
Web: www.troubador.co.uk/matador
Twitter: @matadorbooks

ISBN 978 1803133 102

British Library Cataloguing in Publication Data.
A catalogue record for this book is available from the British Library.

Printed and bound in Great Britain by 4edge Limited
Typeset in 11pt Minion Pro by Troubador Publishing Ltd, Leicester, UK

Matador is an imprint of Troubador Publishing Ltd

Dedicated to Derri, Edward, Rachel
and all the characters I have worked with as a journalist

CHAPTER 1

"It's about time the journalists at this newspaper got off their arses and did some work!" the new Company Secretary said. It was something he said at every opportunity.

Hubert Weaving had been in the building for just over a month. He had arrived unannounced, slipped through a door at the back and sprinted up the stairs that accessed his executive office.

Rumours of a major shake-up had begun to circulate and then, all of a sudden, staff at the *Bridgetown Argus* had their worst fears confirmed. Job losses were on the cards, and journalists were the prime targets.

During the next year, a rash of redundancies, some voluntary, some compulsory, was followed by sackings, a suicide and a fatal heart attack. And every stage of the editorial cull was accompanied by the same message: "The journalists need to get off their arses and do some bloody work!"

Not surprisingly, Hubert Weaving became every journalist's hate figure, and, because of his appearance, he was, among other things, referred to as 'The Dreaded Mister Spock' or 'The Vulcan'.

It was not long before his reputation spread to well beyond the confines of the *Argus* newsroom, and his list of enemies quickly lengthened.

The last time anyone saw him alive was when someone in the building saw him sauntering from the main exit along the lane to the shingled beach. "With a bit of luck, he's on his way to drown himself!" a jaded feature writer had been heard to say.

Among those who heard about 'The Vulcan' was Willard Shakespeare. He made it his business to know, or at least know about, as many people as he could in Bridgetown, a prosperous seaside resort with a population of just under 100,000 and within easy reach of London. The town was big enough to bustle noisily, but not too big to prevent celebrities, business moguls and the gentry from rubbing shoulders with each other and with every kind of crook and miscreant... which is largely why Willard loved it.

Law-makers and law-breakers fascinated Willard, as did the local news gatherers, and meeting them was meat and drink to him. Among those associated with the latter, though hardly regarded as their friend, was Hubert Weaving. Willard had heard plenty about him, but never had the opportunity to meet him.

The news that Weaving had been found bludgeoned to death under a pier had met with mixed reactions. Those who did not know him had been appalled by the brutality involved. Those who did, especially the journalists, undoubtedly felt a sense of relief... though even they had been shaken by the degree of violence involved.

The only clues had been a wallet containing just a book of stamps, a driving licence and a few calling cards found lying nearby. The only DNA to be found belonged to the victim and his wife.

A beleaguered police force had questioned everyone known to have been associated with the victim, including staff at the *Argus*, but had drawn a blank.

Bridgetown had seen a sharp rise in violent crime in recent months, and much of this had been attributed to a 'turf war' between local heavies and a gang from London who were trying to take over control of the local drugs scene. Beatings and stabbings had risen alarmingly in a matter of weeks.

The file on Hubert Weaving's death remained open, but was rarely looked at. The 'turf war' was escalating and the question of who did away with the hated Company Secretary became less pressing and, in many people's minds, was becoming history.

That was not the case with Willard, though. He had heard plenty from the reporters he had encountered in the two pubs that most of them frequented, and he remained consumed with curiosity.

He wanted to know the truth in as much detail as possible, but was aware from past experiences that taking the risk of treading on the toes of the local 'fuzz' could lead to raised hackles and be counter-productive. So, he reluctantly sat on the fence.

Just over two months passed before his tiny office received a surprise visit. The office was at the end of a corridor on the first floor of a two-storey building in a nondescript street. The ground floor was occupied by a firm of insurance brokers. On the first floor, the remaining space was taken up by an advertising agency on one side and a call centre on the other.

A knock on the door to his office, yet to bear his name, was followed almost immediately by a man and a woman bursting in and demanding attention. Willard knew who the woman was straight away and was able to guess the identity of the man.

The woman was Loretta Robey, the glamour model, who had fallen for Hubert Weaving's charms and was now with child following a whirlwind romance. A local celebrity, who had posed and paraded in public almost since puberty, she had married Hubert hurriedly.

Her companion was Sebastian, younger brother of Hubert. He was shorter and rougher-looking than his sibling, and it soon became apparent that he was intellectually inferior.

"It's all very well the police saying they've nothing to go on and that they're inundated with other work, but where does that leave me? I'm pregnant and have no one to support me," she said as she gave Willard a beseeching look.

"It ain't good enough!" Sebastian added.

Willard scratched his head for a moment, before offering to make tea.

"We don't want tea, we want your help and we want the truth!" Sebastian said angrily. Willard detected a hint of menace in the tone.

"What do you think I can do that the police can't?" he asked as calmly and sympathetically as he could.

"You can give us some time, that's what you can do!"

Loretta said. Her tone was bordering on frantic. "You do have the time, don't you?"

Willard had to admit that he did have the time. He did, in fact, have plenty. His senior partner, and before that employer, had died suddenly, and much of the firm's far-from-massive caseload had dried up with the death.

"I don't come cheap," he warned.

"We don't c-care!" Sebastian stuttered. "We just want the truth!"

Willard drew a deep breath and sighed. "All right, I will look into it. I will ask around and see if there is anything, anything at all, the police might have missed," he said. "But I can't make any promises. The police might be over-stretched, but I assure you that they are thorough nonetheless. They are under a lot of pressure and have a lot to cope with, but they do know what they are doing. There's not a lot you can get past them."

He could feel the full force of Sebastian's glare. "Are you scared of doing the job or something?" the younger brother asked with a snarl.

Loretta gave Sebastian a placatory tap on the arm. "Now, now, I'm sure he's not. He's just warning us that what we are asking him to do is not going to be easy. And we already knew that, didn't we?"

Sebastian offered a muted apology.

"Are you prepared to act for us?" Loretta asked Willard again.

Willard nodded. "I will do what I can… as long as you're sure you can afford it, and that you accept that success can't be guaranteed."

CHAPTER 2

Lord Perryman could ignore the facts no longer. His beloved *Bridgetown Argus* was in dire financial straits. Its circulation was plummeting and so, too, was its advertising revenue. The latter had been largely underpinned by the town's estate agents, who, for decades, had used the *Argus* as their main means of publicising properties they had for sale.

Now the estate agents had transferred their allegiances to *The Town Bugle*, a new, free weekly that had quietly set up camp in an unobtrusive backstreet building six months ago. "Their rates are lower and they're offering a far better service," a spokesman for the agents had told Nick Hemsley, the managing director of the *Argus*.

The effect on the paper's finances was going to be cataclysmic, and this latest episode had come in the wake of earlier indications that all was not well at Lord Perryman's flagship newspaper.

Stories of indiscipline, drunkenness, dubious romantic trysts, over-the-top expenses claims and ineffectual management had reached him already.

Something had to be done… a new broom was needed.

Lord Perryman was a man who loved newspapers. He loved the influence that could be brought to bear on all sorts of issues that were important to the public. The production process fascinated him, as did all those involved in every aspect of the industry. The competitive nature of the business, whether it be outselling rival newspapers or being first with the news, had always enthralled him. And, above all, he loved journalists… those talented men and women who sought out material that made news, features or sports stories and produced magical copy with matchless aplomb.

So it was with a heavy heart that he headed for the Wig and Pen for his pre-arranged meeting with Hubert Weaving. The venue was in Fleet Street, the renowned hotbed of the national press before new technology took hold.

It began to occur to him that his choice of meeting place could be seen as anachronistic. Perhaps he should have chosen an alternative location that was in keeping with modern times. Perhaps that was the problem: the press had moved into a new era and it was time for him to keep up with the pace.

That was why he was meeting Weaving, of course.

The young man's reputation had preceded him, and, whether Lord Perryman liked it or not, he seemed to be the man who could provide the cure-all. The proprietor could not avoid a shudder, nonetheless, when the man in question walked in.

Hubert Weaving had just turned thirty. He was six feet tall, slim but strong-looking, with dark hair, coal-black eyes, sallow cheeks and thin lips. His tailor-made pinstripe had been cut to highlight an athletic frame, as did a carefully selected white shirt with blue tie, while his black shoes enabled anyone meeting him to see their reflection in them.

His most distinctive features, though, were pointed ears that resembled those of Mister Spock of *Star Trek*, and of John Redwood, the Conservative politician. He was, of course, well aware that he was widely referred to as 'The Vulcan'.

Lord Perryman bore more than a passing resemblance to Boris Johnson and, in a different set of circumstances, there would have been scope for humour.

In the event, the only words unrelated to business were, "What would you like to drink?" Hubert said he would like a small bitter before the pair sat down together in a corner.

The aristocratic proprietor had donned a pinstripe himself, though he had opted for an open-necked shirt and brown hushpuppies. Hubert eyed him speculatively and came to the rapid conclusion that, despite an initial impression that he was made of the same stuff as P.G. Wodehouse's Bertie Wooster, there was a lot more to him than that. Lord Perryman may have looked like a buffoon, but was anything but. Hubert kept his counsel at the outset and let the man who he hoped would employ him do most of the talking.

"How much do you know about the *Bridgetown Argus*?" Lord Perryman asked.

"Only that it is highly regarded within the profession, and by the public, too," replied Hubert, who had heard plenty already.

Lord Perryman stroked back an imaginary quiff, rubbed his chin and looked at Hubert long and hard.

"It's a newspaper with an excellent reputation… but it has run into problems, I'm afraid," he said at length. Hubert waited for him to continue.

"There is plenty of talent among the journalists and they are a breed of people I have come to admire and respect," the proprietor continued. "But unfortunately talent alone does not always translate into money." Hubert remained impassive and stayed silent.

"The *Argus* has a battery of exceptionally talented people, who write exquisitely and can produce all the material – be it news, features or sport – that the readers could hope to see in a respected provincial newspaper." The proprietor sighed, and Hubert managed to appear inscrutable.

"One of the many problems that needs to be addressed sooner or later is that many of the writers are middle-aged and lacking some of their old fire, and there is a need for new blood. Their output has gone down and their expenses claims have gone up, and the Editor seems to be unwilling or unable to do anything about it. The Editor himself could be part of the trouble, and his actions, or perhaps inactions, need to be monitored. Just as worrying are the reports I have received of a breakdown in discipline. Rumours have reached me of excessive drunkenness, poor timekeeping, various sexual liaisons among members of staff, and even acts of violence."

At this point, Hubert responded by saying: "There clearly needs to be someone there to address these problems."

Lord Perryman noted the absence of emotion and looked into Hubert's eyes. "Yes, the situation is now critical. The paper should never have relied so heavily on just one source of revenue, but I'm afraid that's what's happened."

"What source of revenue are we talking about?" Hubert asked. Having done his homework, he knew the answer already... but decided it was best to let it come from the horse's mouth.

"The estate agents have formed a cartel and collectively withdrawn their advertising support. A new free weekly newspaper, if that's what you can call it, was launched in the town about six months ago. It's called *The Town Bugle*, I believe. Anyway, the people who run it have got the agents to advertise in the *Bugle* instead of the *Argus*."

"How come?" asked Hubert, who, again, knew the answer already.

"By charging much lower rates and providing a much better service," he was told.

"What does your advertising manager have to say about all this?" This time, he did not know.

"Andrew Sumner is no longer with us. My Chief Executive got on to him as soon as we heard the news, and I think it is fair to say he jumped ship before he was pushed!"

"Have you got a replacement?"

Lord Perryman paused, rubbed his chin and looked Hubert straight in the eye. "No, I'm going to stay my hand for the moment. Our first job is to get those property adverts back. Perhaps I should say that ensuring that it happens is going to be one of your first tasks. There's going to be a major shake-up, and you will have to oversee it."

"What about the MD? What will be his role in all this?"

The question was greeted with a long sigh. "Hmm! Nick Hemsley! Nick, dear old Nick, who's been with us for as long as anyone can remember, is approaching retirement and is about to go on a sabbatical."

"Can the company afford to give sabbaticals?" The question was a rash one, and Hubert regretted it immediately.

The response was testy, but tinged with embarrassment. "We probably can't, but it had been arranged long before the latest crisis occurred, and I'm not going back on my word! Please bear in mind what I told you a second ago. He will be retiring soon, and a successor has yet to be named. If you take up the job of Company Secretary, you will be in overall charge for three months shortly after you set foot in the building. How you fare after that is largely in your hands."

There was no fanfare to greet Hubert Weaving on the first day he arrived at the *Bridgetown Argus*. A brief note announcing his appointment as Company Secretary had appeared on various boards, but little notice had been taken.

There was no Nick Hemsley on hand to greet him, and it was left to a senior accounts clerk to welcome him and show him to the office that had hitherto been the domain of the disgraced Andrew Sumner. "I hope you will be happy here," the clerk said, as she handed him a coffee from the nearest vending machine. Hubert thanked her and asked for a sight of the books.

His office was on the top floor of a three-storey building close to the town centre. It was spacious with wall-to-wall carpets, a large pine desk, a leather-bound chair behind it, a separate table and half a dozen wooden chairs ranged along the wall opposite. The walls were bare, though a row of redundant hooks suggested that Sumner, known to be an art lover, had removed several paintings on his departure. A window to one side looked out onto the busy road that accessed the front of the building, and Hubert was quick to realise he was in a position to observe some of the comings and goings outside. Another plus was ease of access to the canteen, a good starting point for assessing the members of staff.

He had yet to meet the MD, the Editor, the Deputy, the Circulation Manager and any of the other executives, though.

The next day, he was invited to the boardroom to meet Nick Hemsley and his personal assistant, Claudine Drew.

The MD, a former barrister, was aristocratic, smartly suited, of average height and, despite his sixty-odd years, possessed an athletic physique. He shook the new employee's hand warmly and apologised for not being around to greet him on arrival.

Claudine Drew was tall, angular with spindly legs and fifty-ish. "Delighted to meet you," she drawled in an American Mid-West accent.

Hubert had already heard that the MD and his aide were more interested in each other than in the *Argus*. Like many others in the firm's employ, he wondered what it was that caused such a stir in Hemsley's loins.

"As you will have heard, I am about to go away for three months and leaving you to hold the fort," the MD said. "I will provide you with contact details in case there are problems and you need to get in touch… though I'm sure you won't." His rich baritone carried with it an air of unmistakable authority. "Before I go, however, I must introduce you to the Editor."

An acquiescent nod served as a cue for the MD to lead Hubert along a corridor and down two flights of stairs to a front reception area. The Editor's office was accessed via two doors to the left of the reception counter. The second door received three vigorous knocks, after which Hemsley marched in at exactly the same time as he was invited to enter.

William Purvis looked up from his desk and rose to his feet with an air of weariness.

"I would like you to meet our newly appointed Company Secretary, Hubert Weaving," the MD told him. "As you know, Hubert will be in charge of finances at the *Argus*, and will be in overall charge while I am away." The two men shook hands.

William Purvis was tallish, at just under six feet, in his late thirties and wore a dark suit, a white shirt with blue stripes and a button undone at the top, and a public-school old boys' tie. His jet-black hair was kept in a quiff and his pallid complexion was beginning to bear worry lines. The sight of the new arrival caused him to blink nervously.

Hubert began to size him up. "Is your Deputy around?" he asked with a wave towards a second desk that faced the one occupied by the Editor.

"I'm afraid he's in hospital having checks on his heart at the moment," Purvis replied. "He hasn't been feeling very well for a while, though he should be back with us in a few weeks."

"That's Graham Wormold," said Hemsley. "He's been at the *Argus* almost since the year dot, and he's now pushing sixty... making him almost as old as me... and the pressure of the job has been getting the better of him lately, I fear."

"Oh dear!" said Hubert, his tone expressionless, his visage inscrutable.

William Purvis tried to soften the gloom by asking the newcomer how he was settling in.

"Oh, finding my feet!" was the languid reply. "At least I know which table they should be under by now!" The Editor tittered. The MD looked nonplussed.

"I will, of course, be taking a good look at how each department here operates, and at whether costs can be cut anywhere," Hubert added, sounding slightly less languid. "I will be wanting to look at the journalists' expenses claims, for example."

CHAPTER 3

It was not hard to see why Jane Smith was the office 'fantasy woman' in the eyes of almost every male member of staff. She was tall, blonde, oval-faced and possessed the sort of slim but rounded figure that could make lorry drivers freeze at the wheel and become a traffic hazard.

She had been moved from the Advertising Department and appointed to the position of Hubert's personal assistant. Hubert could hardly believe his luck.

Hubert, who could not conceal his amusement at the incongruity of her name, was quick to realise that – apart from her obvious assets – she could be used as an unofficial bearer of inside news.

"I hope you realise that a major shake-up is on the way," he told her gravely.

"Oh dear!" Jane replied. "Does that mean my job's on the line?"

"Absolutely not!" he said, though both knew already that there was no need for her to be told. "There's much work to be done to get this company back on its feet and making money again, and you have an important role to play. If you help me in the way I hope you will, you could do very well for yourself." Hubert's expression was inscrutable as ever.

Jane put a hand through her luxuriant hair and smiled. *He's not bad-looking for a Vulcan!* she thought to herself.

"I will try not to let you down," she said aloud.

Hubert now knew that the word 'shake-up' would soon figure in conversations throughout the building. The fact that male journalists and others were frequently prone to leaving their work stations and finding excuses to chat Jane up gave him cause for disapproval, but not surprise, and he could turn the situation to his advantage.

"One of our first priorities is to get back the property advertising," he told her. "Perhaps you could tell me where the *Bugle* office is and who it was who sweet-talked the estate agents into deserting us?"

Jane's hand went up to her hair again. "The person behind the trouble is someone called Shirley Bell, I believe. She's also known as Ginger Bell or Tinker Bell."

"She's certainly cast a spell on a lot of estate agents," Hubert said with a rueful chuckle.

"And she's clearly gingered things up a bit!" Jane quipped with a shrug.

Hubert's eyes narrowed. "Is there anything you know about her?" he asked.

Jane, who realised immediately that there was no more room for humour, responded gravely: "Only that she's in her mid-thirties and divorced… and that within days of her turning up in Bridgetown, the boss at the *Bugle* offered her a job and was quids-in in double-quick time."

A twenty-minute stroll along the seafront could be more than justified. It was as good a way to get to the *Town Bugle* office as any. The air was salty and bracing, the walk along the part that overlooked banks of pebbles was firm underfoot, and Hubert was able to watch incoming waves that caressed the shore rather than crashed into it at the end of their journey. A few families, some with their dogs, sat on the pebble banks, while stridently hungry seagulls hovered hopefully.

A short line of beach huts was left a long way behind as Hubert moved away from Bridgetown's more fashionable parts and headed towards the curiously named Paradise Rest area. Jane had told him to look out for Cable Street, and Hubert wondered if it, in any way, resembled the road of the same name in London's East End.

It was so short and narrow that Hubert almost missed it. To make matters worse, the road sign was grubby and partially obscured by a neglected bramble bush and a cluster of nettles. Cable Street was cobbled, sloped upwards and was flanked by run-down terraced houses and a couple of derelict shops.

The corner with Lisle Lane, where the *Bugle* office was located, was reached almost immediately. A glass-fronted door to a slim detached structure that narrowed at the top bore a new notice indicating that the *Bugle* was at the top, via two staircases. On the ground floor was a small print shop. Half of the first floor was taken by a financial advice firm. The other half was empty.

A steep staircase then led to an attic with a sloping ceiling, newly plastered walls and a floor that had been hurriedly covered with linoleum. A plastic-topped reception counter occupied the space that was once taken up by a door.

A young girl with spiky hair, jeans and a T-shirt rose from a desk and moved forwards to greet the new arrival.

"Are you Shirley Bell?" Hubert enquired.

The girl chuckled. "No, I'm Sharon, assistant to Shirley and to Trevor. Trevor's the boss and he and Shirley are both out just now."

"Are there just the three of you then?"

Sharon beamed. "How did you guess?! Trevor runs things and does the writing, Shirley handles the adverts… and I'm the chief stamp-sticker!"

Hubert offered a sardonic smile. "I'm sure you have them all licked at it!" he quipped. "Any idea where I might find Shirley?"

"Not sure, but it's a pound to a penny she'll be in the town centre chatting up the estate agents."

Hubert, who had guessed that already but wanted to see where the opposition operated from, thanked Sharon and headed back towards the town centre where the agents could be found.

The focal point for building societies, banks and various up-market commercial concerns was Plaza Square, a couple of minutes' walk from the Market Square. Four of the town's estate agency offices could be found at or near one corner. Hubert went into a nearby coffee bar and sat near a window, from which he could observe comings and goings.

No sooner had he sat down and started to sip than he spotted a slim, twin-setted woman emerge from one of the estate agency offices. Her hair was short and ginger, and she was carrying a briefcase. After smiling and waving towards the glass door she had just left behind, she moved purposefully towards another estate agency door.

About half an hour later, Shirley Bell emerged with another wave and the broadest of smiles.

The smile vanished in an instant in the collision that followed and sent her sprawling onto the pavement and led to folders and loose papers flying out of a case that had not been closed properly.

"Oh my goodness!" Hubert exclaimed. "I'm so sorry!" he said as he helped her to her feet and then assisted in the gathering up of folders and papers. "I am so sorry! I was in another world! Are you all right?"

A shaken Shirley nodded.

Hubert, who could sense that he had made an impact in more ways than one by impressing her with his strength, then added: "Is there anything I can do? Can I treat you to a coffee... or perhaps something stronger?"

Shirley hesitated before declining. "That's all right, you don't need to do that," she declared nervously. "I have people to see, anyway."

"Some other time, perhaps?"

Shirley nodded perfunctorily before turning and heading for the next glass door.

Hubert waited to see if she was going to look back before disappearing, and, when she did, he knew he could put the next phase of his strategy into operation. It was purely a matter of timing.

Meanwhile, it was time for him to visit the estate agents himself. Making a point of moving in a direction that ensured his calls would not coincide with those made by Shirley, he quietly, almost meekly, introduced himself to whoever was in charge and tried to glean from the horses' mouths why the agents had switched their allegiances from the *Argus* to the *Bugle*.

It did not take him long to find out. The agents were all of one voice and confirmed what he had heard already. Not only was it far cheaper to advertise with the *Bugle*, but they could also get a vastly superior service.

"The reps at the *Argus* would behave as if they were doing us a favour doing business with us, and they would never put themselves out," one agent commented. "We would hardly ever see them. Shirley, on the other hand, helps us at every stage, every week. She helps us to word the adverts, she will call in to collect them when they're ready, and do everything else in between. If there's any sort of a problem, she will help us fix it. Nothing is ever too much trouble for her." The other agents said much the same.

Hubert, who was well aware that nearly all the agents in the town operated a cartel and made many trading decisions collectively, nodded sympathetically each time.

"She's obviously quite an asset," he would concede.

As he strode back to his new base at the *Argus*, he mused over how best he could put a key part of his strategy into place.

Another pressing matter was that of imposing redundancies, and the questions of how many there should be and who exactly the axe should come down on. All he knew for sure was that the journalists would be bearing the brunt.

Later on, as he pored over the books, in his mission to address these questions, he glanced out of a window just in time to see a man walk towards the *Argus* building from one of the nearby pubs with another man slung over his shoulder. The latter, who was clearly semi-comatose, was the *Argus'* Editor.

CHAPTER 4

"You look as if you could do with a cuppa!" the ever-smiling Sharon said.

Shirley smiled, too, albeit wearily, and nodded. "There ought to be Brownie points for accurate thought-reading," she replied, before taking off her shoes and apologising for such an anti-social action.

"Have no fear!" Sharon replied. "A Sharon Shepley teabag will put the spring back into your step!"

"You really are a thought-reader, aren't you?!" Shirley Bell loved her new job. The salary was far from brilliant and the oft-made greeting of "Here comes Ding Dong!" palled almost as much as the leg work. But her situation since arriving in Bridgetown was an infinite improvement on the previous one. A failed marriage, an acrimonious divorce and the need to distance herself from the threats of an abusive ex-husband were hopefully well behind her.

"There you go!" Sharon said as she plonked a steaming mug on to Shirley's desk. "Get it down you!"

A few grateful sips followed, after which Shirley asked if

there had been any messages.

"Oh, just the usual one or two from agents wanting to alter their ads slightly. Nothing big, though."

"That's a relief! So nothing else, then?"

Sharon was about to say 'No' when she remembered a visit from a stranger and two subsequent telephone calls.

"What was his name?"

Sharon scratched her spiky head. "I think it was Hughroy Wheatley, or Wheating… something like that, anyway. Said 'e was new in town."

"Any idea what he wanted? What was he like?"

"I don't know what he wanted, 'cept that he wanted to talk to you. He was tallish, youngish and smartish. A bit of all right, really, though he had big pointy ears that made him look like Mister Spock, I suppose. Yes, that's it. He looked like Mister Spock."

The news seemed to perk Shirley up. "I've always wanted to be pursued by a Vulcan!" she quipped. Sharon chuckled. "Did he say he'd call back?"

Hubert had another matter to attend to first. It concerned the newspaper's philandering Chief Photographer and his female assistant. The sexual exploits of Harry Phillipson were legendary. During his fifteen years as a talented 'snapper', he was known to have had four affairs with young women employed at the *Argus*, three barmaids, and at least three housewives he had visited ostensibly to photograph. The silver-tongued lothario, now in his mid-fifties, had somehow managed to keep his wife in the dark.

His twenty-two-year-old assistant, Lynette Coe, was married, too. A former model, she had turned up for duties every day wearing the shortest of skirts that highlighted long, slim legs and white frilly knickers.

The male members of staff were not slow to notice, of course, but, as usual, it was Harry Phillipson who took the initiative first.

But this time, there was a difference. Lynette's husband, Kevin, a professional footballer with a tendency to mistrust people at the best of times, had grown suspicious. "Why can't I ever get you on the phone on the days I'm playing away?" he had asked more than once. His wife's denial that anything untoward could possibly be going on had been accompanied by ridicule.

The doughty Fourth Division defender had been kept quiet for a time… but not for much longer.

Then, one day, a cancelled away fixture saw a disgruntled Kevin Coe head home early. A phone call home had been fruitless, and Kevin decided there and then to go straight to the *Argus* as soon as he was back in Bridgetown.

By the time he got there, it was after 5pm and all but a handful of staff had gone home. Kevin knew that the quickest route to the photographers' work station was via a single flight of stairs at the back. As he neared the top of the flight, he heard a sound that strengthened his worst fears.

The opening of a door gave him the sight of his wife lying spread-eagled across a table and the Chief Photographer, trousers at half mast, making love to her.

The commotion that followed quickly reached the ears of an already suspicious Hubert, who went to see what was going on. After ordering Kevin, who was busy battering Harry, to leave or face the police, he sacked the two miscreants on the spot.

The following Monday morning, a memo emanating from the Saturday tryst was circulated to all departments. It made it clear that such behaviour would not be tolerated, and would lead to instant dismissal. The memo also referred to the company being in financial trouble, and stated that the staff needed to pull their socks up... and that redundancies were likely in the near future.

William Purvis went ashen when Hubert marched into his office, told the Editor why the chief photographer and his assistant had been dismissed, and then expressed amazement that the matter had not been nipped in the bud before it got out of hand.

"This has been going on for some time, hasn't it?" Hubert asked pointedly, before leaving the Editor to contemplate his future.

As it happened, Purvis had relatives in high places in the form of an uncle who headed up a brewery chain and a cousin who had just been appointed Editor of a national newspaper. The post of Deputy Editor beckoned and, now that the sea air had lost much of its charm, the offer of the post was readily accepted.

Hubert made one attempt to inform Nick Hemsley that the *Argus* would soon be without an Editor, but found him to be incommunicado. He then contacted Lord Perryman, who instructed him to advertise for a replacement urgently.

He then compiled his first redundancy list. It consisted of the names of four journalists, a cuttings librarian and a messenger. His subsequent announcement bore the warning that other job losses would be needed to make the newspaper solvent once more.

News that all was not well at the *Argus* spread rapidly. One of the first to hear it was Graham Wormold, the Deputy Editor, who had left hospital and was convalescing in Cyprus. "You need plenty of rest and no stress," the heart specialist had told him.

Six weeks in a luxury hotel in Paphos seemed to be the perfect tonic. Sun-kissed shores, deck chairs aplenty, substantial and succulent meals, gentle evening strolls and natives who nearly always spoke fluent English were meat and drink to him. So, too, was the ease of access to a Martini, though this, along with the heavy meals, had not been prescribed. However, it was not in his nature to argue with an order to rest.

When his wife, Eileen, told him William Purvis was on the phone and anxious to talk to him, he experienced a sinking feeling and a quickening of the pulse. He had no option but to lift his plump body from a chair by the side of a swimming pool and take the call.

"I think you ought to know that I am about to leave the *Argus*," his boss told him. The customary urbane preamble was conspicuous by its absence.

Graham Wormold's pulse gathered pace again. "Oh!" he replied with a gulp.

"I have been offered a plum job on *The Times* and it seems silly for me not to take it."

"Oh!"

"You sound startled, Graham! I'm really sorry. Believe me, I have enjoyed working with you and I hope we can stay in touch. But I have decided it's time to move on, and I might well be gone by the time you get back."

Graham offered an unconvincing, "Congratulations and good luck," before hanging up and sitting in a nearby hotel foyer chair with his head in his hands.

"What's the matter, darling?" Eileen asked after sidling up to him.

"I feel giddy," her husband replied. Then, after hardly a pause, he added: "I have to go back."

Eileen tried to dissuade him, but to no avail, and they were on a plane the next day. They had been in Paphos for just over two weeks.

Eileen did all she could to give her husband peace of mind on the homeward journey, and, later on, in their sitting room. But it was hopeless. Her husband was terse, tense, snappy and, at times, seemed breathless. Her plea for him not to worry and saying, "We will get through whatever lies ahead together," was met with an angry response. "Shut up! What do you know about it?!" She had never seen him like this.

The night was no better. Sleep came in small doses, interspersed with Graham pacing round each room and Eileen listening anxiously. Breakfast was a hurried affair, though Eileen was heartened by her husband's ability to maintain his appetite. Bacon, eggs and sausages, followed by toast, marmalade and a massive mug of coffee, were consumed with customary relish.

The drive from home to the *Argus* began at the usual hour, too. Graham did not like to start work too early, or finish too late for that matter, and Eileen was relieved to see the customary pattern continue. And the journey to work went as smoothly as could be hoped.

It was not until he reached the newspaper company's cramped car park that matters began to grow pear-shaped.

Car-parking spaces had always only been available to key staff at the *Argus*. Apart from the Editor and Deputy, they were allocated to the Managing Director, Company Secretary, Advertising Manager, Works Manager, Head of Circulation and four or five others considered to be of executive status.

Graham Wormold's heart missed a beat when he saw his space occupied by a yellow Citroen, the make of car he knew was now being awarded to those thought to be deserving. He cursed under his breath. There was nothing for it but to take his slightly battered Mercedes to a spot that was ten minutes' walk away.

His first port of call on returning to the *Argus* building was the Editor's office. "He isn't in yet," a girl he had never seen before told him. He then went to the boardroom, only to be reminded that the MD was enjoying a sabbatical abroad.

"Hubert Weaving, the new Company Secretary, is the person you need to see," another girl at a nearby desk told him. He did not recognise her, either.

The voluptuous Jane Smith was known to him, of course, though even she had assumed a new role is his absence, he discovered. "I will see if he is available," she said, reaching for a telephone. She offered a smile that was wide, warm and predatory all at once. "Mr Weaving will be free to see you shortly," she informed Graham.

Ten minutes elapsed before he asked if there was anywhere he could sit while waiting. Jane Smith got up, went to a table that lay between her desk and the door to Hubert Weaving's office and found a stool. "There you go, try this," she said stonily.

Graham perched himself on the stool and began to mull over his lengthy career. It had been underpinned by charm, an ability to say things people liked to hear and a knack of obtaining plaudits for results emanating from the efforts of others. His ability to ride office storms and remain unruffled was something else that gave him immense satisfaction.

Another ten minutes went by, and then another ten, and there was still no sign of the new Company Secretary being available to speak to him.

Graham asked Jane if Mr Weaving would be ready shortly and, after another phone call, was told: "He won't be much longer."

The Deputy Editor got off his stool and then back on again in an attempt to get more comfortable. He cast his mind back to the day when, at the behest of the Editor, he took a journalist who turned out to be an alcoholic to a drying-out clinic and, because of his florid complexion, was mistakenly thought to be the patient. It was an incident that enabled him to smile inwardly.

After a total of forty-five minutes, the phone rang and Jane announced that Mr Weaving was now able to see him.

An imperious "Come!" followed his knock on the door and, on entering, Graham was astonished to discover that the man he was confronting was barely half his age.

"I have been informed of your complaint and am afraid I'm going to have to tell you some unpalatable home truths," the new Company Secretary informed him.

Graham Wormold felt a tightness around the chest and a feeling of giddiness. In the absence of an invitation to take a seat, he found a chair and plonked himself on it. Hubert Weaving glared at him as he did so.

"We are now only allocating car-parking spaces to people who make money for the company," he said with a hint of a sneer.

The Deputy Editor's florid face turned a deep crimson.

"That's outrageous!" he spluttered. "I have done all sorts of things for the company. I have worked here for over twenty years, and done so with unstinting loyalty. What you have said is beyond the pale!"

Hubert Weaving's eyes narrowed and the curl in his lip became more pronounced. "I am very sorry, but that's how it is!" he said. "We need people who make us money! We're keeping a space open for the Editor for the time being, but we might have to review that later on as well. The truth of the matter is, whether you like it or not, the company is in financial trouble and there have to be changes... drastic changes. One of the most immediate of these is that the journalists are going to have to get off their arses and do some bloody work!"

CHAPTER 5

"What's up?" Cicely asked on hearing a sigh that followed the sound of the latest *Argus* issue descending on her boss's desk.

"I guess it's a case of whereby the grace of God goes I," Willard replied gravely.

"Oh dear! Who's died?" As usual, there was no beating about the bush with Cicely.

Willard sighed again. "Do you remember meeting Graham Wormold, the Deputy Editor of the *Argus*?"

"Oh yes, the one who looks like a walking heart attack! I've met him once… at that recent cocktail do."

Willard winced. "That's the one," he said. "He has just died… of a heart attack!"

Now it was Cicely's turn to wince. "Oh, my goodness!" she said with a gulp. Then, after an uncharacteristic pause, she asked falteringly: "Was there anything in particular that brought it on?"

"It looks as if there was," she was told. Willard went on to recount how a reporter at the *Argus* had described the scandal emanating from Wormold losing his car-parking space on his return to work after being off sick.

"Poor old Derek practically blew a gasket, by all accounts. After storming home in a state of high dudgeon, he tried to contact the MD… only to learn that he was on a sabbatical with the paramour who passed as an assistant!"

"Goodness gracious!"

"He then took his protest to the proprietor – Lord Perryman, I think his name is – and, when he couldn't get him on the phone, he drove straight to London, barged into the club where he happened to be at the time and registered his anger in front of anyone who happened to be within earshot."

"That must have cost him a lot of sympathy," Cicely suggested.

"Yes, but not for long," Willard said. "Lord Perryman was initially put out, of course, but it did not take him long to realise that something was seriously wrong, and, after looking into the matter, he ordered Weaving to give Wormold his parking space back."

"I hope that Weaving chap got a good telling-off for the way he behaved. He sounds a thoroughly nasty piece of work."

"Me, too. I couldn't agree more."

"I've heard that Lord Perryman has a love of journalists," Cicely observed. "I have also heard that Weaving has a number of nicknames, the most common one being 'The Vulcan'. It amazes me that Perryman would want to employ someone like Weaving."

"I've heard that, too. One thing's for sure. Perryman would not employ someone like him unless he really had to."

"So, what happened exactly?"

Willard sighed again. "I'm afraid that the whole business was too much for poor old Derek," he said. "It took a few days to resolve, I believe, and Derek became increasingly agitated and het up. Lord Perryman did eventually get back to Derek and told him he could have his parking space back, apparently, but the damage had been done. The morning after hearing the good news, Derek went to his garage, got into his car and then had a massive heart attack while starting to drive to work."

"I should imagine everyone at the *Argus* is in a state of shock!"

"I dare say they are, but that doesn't alter the fact that there's already speculation over who's going to be given Derek's job... and whether his replacement will get that parking space, for that matter." Willard could not suppress a wry smile.

Cicely followed suit. "I have always believed that the newspaper business is pretty cut-throat, but is it really as bad as that?"

"I rather fear it can be," Willard replied. He then looked at his watch and, on seeing it was half past twelve, suggested that now was a good time for his doughty assistant to take a lunch break.

The departure of Cicely gave Willard the opportunity to reflect. He had got to know Derek Wormold well over the years, having shared many a pint with him in one or other of the two hostelries the journalists at the *Argus* liked to frequent.

It had soon become apparent after their first encounter that the former Deputy Editor was a master raconteur with a penchant for blue jokes. There was no doubting that Willard enjoyed Derek's company, which was highly amusing, though he could also see that Derek's other talents included an ability to say what others wanted to hear and an adroitness at garnering credit for efforts strenuously carried out by others.

He had got to know many of the other journalists, too, and could see that, while Derek's status at the *Argus* ensured that he received courtesy from minions, there was a subtle absence of trust. This was partly due to his ability to prune expenses claims… a role he had taken over from the Editor and one which earned him a few Brownie points from the board of directors.

Among the journalists he had got to know better were the philandering photographer Harry Phillipson and the fiery, irascible Chief Reporter Hamish McLennan.

Harry's sexual exploits were legendary. Barmaids at both pubs would give each other knowing looks whenever he entered. Many of the barmaids were cash-strapped students employed on a temporary basis, who, before long, received a new dimension to their education. Some of Harry's conquests were housewives, who were, ostensibly at least, visited for professional reasons. Others, inevitably, were colleagues… with reporters, advertising reps, receptionists and canteen staff all falling under his spell. The sacking of Harry, when it eventually occurred, came as no surprise to Willard.

Hamish, who was still employed at the *Argus*, was no less colourful. Rough, tough and bearded, he had a nose for news that was second to none and a tendency to settle arguments with his fists. At least two of his colleagues knew this to their cost. And, although married with five children, he was not averse to 'playing away' either. Firstly, he had an affair with a news desk secretary and then he forsook her for a tall, leggy copy-taker who turned out to be a blow job expert. Her name was Jackie.

Their affair was anything but a well-kept secret, and, for a time, the pair seemed to be inseparable. Not only did Hamish and Jackie appear together at almost every social function involving local journalists, but they were forever being seen canoodling in public… and they could not even keep their hands off each other in the newsroom.

One day, their not-so-private trysts attracted the unwanted attention of Barry Miles, a telex operator and known peeping Tom, who, one evening, watched the pair make love in a parkland spinney. Hamish caught Barry at it and battered him so badly that he needed several days off work afterwards.

Not long after that, Hamish's wife heard about the incident and threatened to start divorce proceedings. Meanwhile, Jackie had begun to switch her attention to a middle-aged accounts clerk and been seen giving him the 'full treatment' in his office.

Hamish's demeanour darkened noticeably for a while after that, and word got round the newsroom that anyone speaking out of turn would do so at their peril. Many of the journalists at the time were prone to getting drunk during lunchtime, and it was perhaps a miracle that none of them said a word out of place in Hamish's presence.

Among those who liked to imbibe to excess was the *Argus'* Editor, William Purvis, and there were said to have been several occasions when Hamish had been seen carrying him over his shoulder while walking from the Rose and Crown to their workplace.

Willard did not know the *Argus'* Editor well, though he had heard that, while he could be benevolent towards his staff, he was lazy, ineffectual and the object of contempt among many… most notably Hamish McLennan.

Willard then began to reflect on his own life and how he ended up as an enquiry agent in Bridgetown.

As he so often did, he mused over the fact that his poor academic record, especially when it came to English, made him the butt of jokes in school classrooms. The fact that he was mildly dyslexic eventually came to light, though this did nothing to stop the jokes. Not surprisingly perhaps, the incongruity of his name was a source of hilarity. When it became known he was dyslexic, there were repeated attempts to derive fun from distorting his name and calling him something else. Among the favourites were Spearshake, Darwill, Shakepears, Swillyard and, most frequently of all, Willyshake. Catcalls would accompany the teasing and, had it not been for the fact that Willard was both big for his age and slow to anger, the playground scraps would not have been so occasional as they were. Willard was, in fact, able to see the funny side himself, and managed to become a popular figure rather than a figure of fun.

A far bigger challenge for Willard was what to do after leaving school. This was followed by a spell in the Army, which saw him rise to the rank of corporal. However, he quickly came to the conclusion that such a regimented life was not for him, and he bought himself out. A series of civilian roles followed, including door-to-door selling, market research and night security, but none of them ticked the right boxes. Eventually he found himself on the dole and with a seemingly bleak and uncertain future.

It was purely by chance that he found, or, to be precise, literally tumbled on his true vocation. A chain of events began with him tripping over a despatch case in Bridgetown's busy shopping centre. After cursing and dusting himself down, Willard noticed a man lying on a nearby bench. The man was clasping his chest and clearly in distress. Willard had the presence of mind to get a passer-by to ring for an ambulance while he applied CPR, something he had learned in the Army.

The ambulance whisked the man away and, the following day, Willard, who hated mysteries at the best of times, made a point of finding out where and how he was. And it was this that led him to meeting Jim and Hilary Carter, proprietors of 'Carter's, Enquiry Agents'.

Ex-policeman Jim was back in his office within a couple of weeks, despite pleas from his wife to take a much longer rest. Jim did, however, recognise the need for someone else to relieve him of some of the leg work. He wanted Hilary to continue in her part-time secretarial capacity, and did not want to expose her to any dangers, real or imagined, that she might encounter on the outside.

The job of 'part-time leg man' was offered to Willard, who was delighted to accept. It was a role he had dreamed about but not entertained seriously, and he fell into immediately and easily. As Jim's health continued to deteriorate and Willard's investigative flair became increasingly apparent, it was not long before the new recruit became a full-time employee. A junior partnership followed a couple of years later. And, when Jim died, a year after that, Hilary stayed on and she and Willard eventually became equal partners, with Willard operating on the outside and Hilary continuing as secretary and providing much-needed assistance with the reading of letters and documents.

The next stage of the partnership was to re-name it Carter and Shakespeare.

CHAPTER 6

"Hello, it's me!"

"Who's me?"

"It's me! Hubert! The guy you literally bumped into the other day."

"If I remember correctly, it was *you* who bumped into *me!*" Shirley Bell did her best to sound vaguely frosty, though, in reality, her pulse was racing. She had hoped he would get in touch, and when she heard his cultured, sonorous voice on the telephone, the idea of trying to sound detached was something of a challenge. "To what do I owe this honour?" she asked as coolly as she could.

"I understand that the annual Bridgetown Businessmen's Ball takes place this Saturday, and I am wondering if you would care to accompany me," Hubert said.

Shirley's pulse went into overdrive. "Did you say *this* Saturday?" she asked after a moment's hesitation.

"Yes, it's definitely this Saturday. I understand that it's one of Bridgetown's most prestigious events and, as a newcomer to the town, I am keen to go. Unfortunately, though, I have no one to go with, and you would be doing me an honour if you agreed to partner me for the evening."

"That's very flattering! Give me a minute while I consult my diary." Shirley, who had an open diary showing a blank page for Saturday in front of her, paused for a moment and rustled the paper a couple of times before replying, "That seems to be fine. Thank you very much."

Hubert expressed delight and promised to 'put on his best bib and tucker'.

Keeping his promise entailed a visit to a local gentlemen's outfitter, who provided him with evening wear that was both elegant and physique-enhancing. Hubert was in an upbeat frame of mind by the time the big evening arrived. Two members of the editorial staff at the *Argus* had suddenly got itchy feet and resigned. A third had been caught fiddling his expenses and was due for the high jump.

Shirley had been to an outfitter, too. The shop assistant serving her had drawn her attention to a striking scarlet dress that was low-cut and had a slit down one side. The idea of impressing Hubert with a display of cleavage and thigh almost tempted her. However, she decided to be a little more discreet and instead opted for a little black number that showed her figure to advantage, but less obviously.

The doorbell of her flat rang at exactly the time she was told it would. "Your carriage awaits!" her smiling suitor told her. The sight of a Rolls-Royce with a chauffeur at the wheel made her give a start. Hubert gazed at her for a couple of seconds and smiled again. "Only the best for you!" he declared.

It had been a long time since Shirley last sensed that she was being wooed and about to be seduced, and the feeling was by no means unpleasant!

As always, the annual Bridgetown Businessmen's Ball was held in the Town Hall. It had been an annual event for as long as anyone could remember and the only recent change to its format was to recognise that women were capable of running businesses as well as men. Until three years ago, it had been assumed that all women attending were either wives or girlfriends. The name of the event had yet to be changed, though proposals to call it the Business Ball, Business Persons' Ball or Business Men's and Women's Ball had been put to the council.

As always, uniformed security staff were at the entrance and inside, and those attending the ball joined cloakroom queues before handing over their outdoor coats and being issued with tickets under the scrutiny of the head cloakroom attendant. The attendants were invariably volunteers and tended to be retired police officers. At other times of the year, the cloakrooms had a run-down look to them. However, for the big day, they were always scrupulously cleaned and given a new lick of paint.

The main council chamber, which had a stage at one end and an area earmarked for dancing in front of it, had been the scene of feverish activity while it was made as pristine as possible.

There was table space for five hundred. The tables, of varying sizes, were nearly all allocated according to job or profession. The *Bridgetown Argus* had one of the smaller tables, while, not far away, was a rather larger one reserved for the town's estate agents. Banks, building societies, insurance companies, solicitors, retailers and hoteliers were among those occupying other tables.

The top table was always occupied by the mayor, mayoress, other council dignitaries and guests of honour who might include stars from the world of sport or showbusiness. It continued to be close to the band on the stage, despite attempts to 'move away from that infernal noise.'

A battery of waiters in evening dress and waitresses in cocktail dresses lined three walls.

Hubert had hoped to secure a table for two so that he could be assured of Shirley's undivided attention. There were none, however, and the pair ended up on the *Argus* table. The places allocated to them happened to see them sitting opposite Jane Smith and her latest beau. Jane, whose dress was just as red and revealing as the one that Shirley had rejected, was so much the centre of attention that Hubert's presence was seen as unobtrusive.

There were just a dozen seats at the *Argus* table. The seats were usually coveted, but, on this occasion, four were empty and the other four were occupied by an advertising rep and an accounts clerk with their respective spouses. Hubert and Shirley were at one end with Jane and her beau, while the others kept their distance at the other end.

Jane's beau, whose name turned out to be Peter, informed Hubert that he was a bank clerk. His conversation bordered on monosyllabic, but, as Shirley said later, he was tall, dark and devastatingly handsome. "Peter will introduce you to his boss, Mr Allsopp, this evening, if he gets the chance," Jane told Hubert. "He's at the bankers' table and, when it comes to matters of finance, he has his ear to the ground."

"It sounds as if your ear is in much the same place!" said Hubert. "I'm impressed!" He appreciated that cultivating Mr Allsopp would be worth his while. The same could be said for cultivating Jane. His immediate priority, however, was to woo and impress Shirley.

"Are you sitting comfortably?" he asked the lady from the *Bugle* with a wink.

Shirley smiled coyly. "Yes, I'm fine," she said. "It's nice here. I've heard the ball is a good do, and it certainly seems to be so far."

"It's very good," Jane told her from across the table. "This is the third time I've been here, and you can take it from me you're going to have a good time." Jane was, of course, well aware who she was, and it did not take her long to guess what her new boss was up to.

The first course arrived, and Hubert was quick to declare that its quality more than lived up to expectations. It was, in fact, prawn cocktail surrounded by lettuce with salad cream and housed in an ornate glass. Hubert asked Shirley if it was to her liking. Shirley smiled and confirmed that it was, and Hubert initiated a discussion on good food and where to get it. Jane was quick to join in. "My favourite eating place is Brown's," she said. "It's pricey, but there's no lack of quality, or quantity for that matter… What's your favourite eating place, Peter?"

Her beau nodded, grunted and said something like, "Yes."

For the second course, diners could choose from a selection of meat and fish dishes plus a couple of vegan options. "This is great, isn't it?" Jane said to Shirley. A wine waiter appeared to top up everyone's glasses, and Shirley agreed with a sip that the occasion was 'top drawer'. Hubert gave Shirley's hand a gentle squeeze and said: "That's really good to hear." A reflexive reciprocal squeeze followed.

Shirley took a second sip, followed quickly by a third, between mouthfuls of the best halibut she had ever tasted. Hubert tucked into a rump steak with the enthusiasm of a wolf that had just caught its prey after a long hunt. He continued to talk to Jane, Peter and Shirley about food in general, and encouraged the latter in particular to enjoy her meal and to not neglect the wine.

The third course had options, too. Hubert and Shirley both decided to eschew the puddings and savour the peaches and cream. Coffee, mints and a glass of champagne for everyone present followed, during which the town mayor gave his customary speech of welcome, with a quick review of what had occurred in Bridgetown during the last twelve months, before introducing the guest of honour.

On this occasion, it was the celebrated cricketer Ben Potter. A larger-than-life character, whose off-the-pitch exploits were as well documented as his achievements on the field, he regaled guests with a series of side-splitting anecdotes. The speaker, whose liking for liquor more than matched that of the other diners, was regaled with cheers that continued for several minutes after he had finished.

The band then took over, and the charismatic cricketer took to the floor for a quickstep with his young wife Angie, a fashion model. Other diners followed suit and, before long, those who remained seated were in the minority. Jane half-cajoled, half-dragged Peter to his feet and joined in with inelegant gusto. Hubert and Shirley stayed put for a while.

"That's interesting," said Hubert. "I would have guessed that Jane was a good dancer, but, in fact, she's a bit ungainly, don't you think?"

Shirley smiled widely, almost grinned. "Yes, she is a bit. What about yourself? You sound as if you know something about it."

Hubert told Shirley that he learned to dance at the age of sixteen. "How come? Who taught you?" Shirley asked.

"It all started on the day I discovered girls," he said. "I was very shy and gauche at the time."

"I find that hard to believe… but do tell me more!" said Shirley, who really was grinning now.

"My younger sister was at the house of a schoolfriend at the other end of the road that we lived in and my parents asked me to go and collect her because it was past her bedtime," said Hubert. "The friend's older sister, who was the same age as me but far more mature, answered the door and said, 'Hello Hubert!' so warmly that I was blown away. I remember to this day that she was wearing a tight-fitting pink jumper—"

"And that had nothing to do with it, of course?!"

"Now now now!" said Hubert, placing a hand on one of Shirley's knees and letting it stay there for a second or two. Shirley, who showed no signs of objecting, asked him to continue his story.

"The trouble was that I couldn't find the courage to ask her out. I knew nothing about girls, and had no idea how to go about it anyway."

"You must have been at an all-boys' school!"

"You are quite right. How did you guess?! That doesn't alter the fact that, from then on, I was thinking about her in the classroom all the time, and, when not at school, I was constantly on the lookout for a sighting of her. Eventually I plucked up the courage to go to her house and ask if I could borrow her logarithm tables. I told her I had mislaid my own and needed them urgently for my maths homework."

"That sounds a novel approach. You were well and truly logged in, weren't you!"

Hubert chuckled. "It was the best I could do at the time, and it might well have helped do the trick. For, a few days after I had gratefully returned the log tables, she invited me – via my sister – to partner her at her school's annual dance."

"Was that when you learned to dance?"

"Absolutely! I didn't have a clue at the time. So, I joined a local dancing class and, by the time the school dance took place a few weeks later, I had at least some idea of how to do it."

"How did the romance go?" The normally pensive Shirley was now grinning more broadly than ever.

Hubert offered a wry smile. "It was all right, in a very chaste way for a while, but I was still hopelessly shy. After not all that long, she forsook me for a mature man of eighteen!"

Shirley uttered a sympathetic "Aaah!" and gave Hubert a gentle thigh squeeze. She could not recall when she had last made such a gesture. Hubert reciprocated and suggested it was time for them to do some dancing of their own.

Most of the rest of the evening was spent gyrating, gliding and smooching as the band went through its repertoire. Hubert was a more than competent dancer. Shirley was an expert, which was largely why they moved in sync so easily. Hubert was quick to acknowledge her skills, and Shirley told him that, in the distant past, she had danced professionally and, later on, run a school for those wanting to learn. Hubert came close to asking her how she ended up being involved with estate agents, but reminded himself that talking shop was out at present.

Towards the end of the evening, the lights went low and the tempo of the music slowed. Shirley pressed her body against his, and Hubert kissed her lingeringly but gently on the mouth. There was no longer any doubt that the rivals in business were about to become lovers.

The chauffeur was waiting outside when it was time to leave. Shirley was taken to her front door, and Hubert kissed her again. Shirley did not invite him in, though. Not this time. And Hubert did not suggest that she should. There was, after all, a need to observe decorum.

"Thank you for a lovely evening," Shirley said before closing her door.

"See you soon," her suitor replied as she did.

CHAPTER 7

Paperwork was nothing but anathema to Willard. So, too, was chasing up bills, not to mention receiving them. Willard would have hated these disciplines even if he was not dyslexic, though having to read what was in front of him hardly helped.

So, when the prim and proper Cicely turned up out of the blue and expressed a desire to 'work for a private eye… and I don't expect to be paid much', she was soon snapped up.

It quickly transpired that Cicely's main passions in life were solving mysteries, keeping things in apple pie order and ensuring the utmost efficiency in any operations in which she was involved.

Hilary had become more and more a sleeping partner who provided finance when needed, and was rarely around to help with paperwork in the way she had helped her late husband, and Willard could hardly believe his luck.

The new recruit was in her early- to mid-fifties, small, skinny and mouse-like in appearance. She had protruding teeth and wore horn-rimmed spectacles. She was contracted to work mornings only, but was so dedicated to her role that she often remained in the office until well into the afternoon.

Willard sensed that Cicely was keen to keep him in order, as well as the office, and had no complaints about this. She was probably right to do so!

Another of Cicely's assets was that, although she was a spinster living alone in a sleepy hamlet a few miles to the north of Bridgetown, she seemed to have her ear close to the ground and match Willard's ability to keep tabs on local gossip.

This was almost as useful as Willard being introduced to the concept of filing. Perhaps for the first time in his life, he recognised the merit of having, as Cicely put it, 'everything in its proper place'.

Cicely's arrival coincided with the virtual departure of Hilary, whose interest in the business had diminished rapidly after the death of her beloved Jim. Hilary, who had always worked mainly in a secretarial capacity, had talked of pulling out of her partnership with Willard, so Willard faced an uncertain future.

However, at least there was now someone who could sort out the filing and answer the phone. All that was needed was a client or two!

Willard's latest case had entailed tracing a family heirloom, a brooch with little intrinsic worth but of great sentimental value. It ended when his customer found it the next day under an armchair in her sitting room.

His only existing client was a Mr Forsdyke, who was constantly convinced that his wife was being unfaithful to him. He had inherited him from Jim, and looked upon him as an on-and-off client.

Aubrey Forsdyke had been one of the first to contact the Carters, expressing a desire to have his wife watched and 'never mind the expense'. Jim Carter's initial five-day vigil proved fruitless, and Mr Forsdyke was told she had not left the house except to go shopping. Mr Forsdyke was persuaded that there was nothing else to be done, but that did not prevent him from reappearing every two to three months to seek checks on her perceived transgressions.

Willard viewed these visits with a degree of ambivalence. They were no longer a source of faint amusement, and he regarded them as tedious. Like Jim Carter before him, he had tactfully advised Mr Forsdyke not to waste his time and money. However, there was no escaping the fact that the waste of time was helping to keep his business afloat! And, by the law of averages, another Forsdyke visit was imminent!

Meanwhile, Willard was musing over reports he had heard about the latest cull at the *Argus*. Seven members of staff who were in their fifties were being offered early retirement packages. Five of the seven were journalists and three were feature writers who had, over the years, amassed a hatful of awards for the quality of their work.

A new Editor and Deputy Editor has been appointed to replace Purvis and Wormold, and one of their first tasks was to ensure that the journalists being offered retirement deals accepted them. "If you don't accept, there will almost certainly have to be redundancies," they were told. It was just a matter of time before they all succumbed to pressure.

The other priority was, of course, to help with the wooing of the estate agents and getting them to advertise in the *Argus* once more.

The new Editor was Kelvin Watson, a thrusting, blunt-talking Yorkshireman in his early thirties, who criticised his predecessor without naming him at every opportunity and declared that changes for the better were on the way. He did not specify what the improvements would be, but assured his staff that there would be a better newspaper, a new work ethic and no room for 'ego trips'. Long, convoluted features were to be consigned to the past and be replaced with material bought in from press agencies.

It soon became apparent that he was a champion of clean living, and he strongly disapproved of both alcohol and tobacco. However, in not wanting to appear unduly prissy, he swore copiously.

His Deputy, Andy McCallum, was a tall, thin Scot who had just passed thirty. A former trade union activist, he had 'crossed the floor' and was now able to pass on useful information to management on how rebellious staff behaved and how to deal with them. He had abandoned his liking for beer and whisky even more quickly than he had his left-wing opinions. He spoke little, but carried with him an aura of menace that matched his ability to dot i's and cross t's.

News of these latest changes first reached Willard via Cicely, who would not say how she knew about them.

They were confirmed later in the King's Head by Hamish McLennan. The Chief Reporter was seething with anger. "It's just a matter of time before I punch someone's fucking head in!" he told Willard. The main source for his ire was Hubert 'The Fucking Vulcan' Weaving, though he was none too fond either of the new Editor and his Deputy.

Another rumour doing the rounds was that Weaving was wooing 'that dreaded ginger bitch at the *Bugle*'. Willard had heard this from one of the feature writers who was under the cosh and from Cicely, too. Not surprisingly, there was speculation regarding Weaving's exact motives.

"You seem to be a font of all knowledge," Willard had told Cicely. "You never fail to surprise me!"

Willard was wondering, in hindsight, whether he should have kept such an observation to himself, when who should appear through the door but the bulky form of Aubrey Forsdyke.

"I think I have got her at last!" the visitor announced.

CHAPTER 8

"What makes you think that?" Willard asked. His heart was sinking and soaring at almost the same time. If there was ever a perfect example of ambivalence, this was it. The prospect of being employed once more to stalk someone like Estelle Forsdyke did not thrill him at all. But he needed the money!

"Do sit down," he said wearily. "I take it you still believe your wife is being unfaithful." Aubrey Forsdyke plonked himself down on the chair closest to Willard's desk and nodded, impervious to the tone Willard had been unable to disguise.

"Are you sure?" Willard asked. "Do you have a reason to go against the advice you have been given in the past?"

"I do."

The answer was met with a sigh. "Are you absolutely sure? Remember, you have got me, and my former boss for that matter, to follow your wife and see what she has got up to several times already, and I can only repeat what I have said before... I don't believe your wife has done anything untoward." Willard felt duty-bound to say it as he saw it, whatever the financial considerations were.

Aubrey Forsdyke continued to appear agitated, and it quickly became apparent that he was not going to be denied. "All right, you had better tell me about it," Willard then said.

Aubrey appeared to be hurt by the implied suggestion that he was not being taken seriously. He was, after all, a serious man. He was a deeply religious man, too, and could be deeply moved by both acts of faith and perceived transgressions. Now in his early forties, he had been a Christian all his life. He had been married to a much younger woman, who had become pregnant three times and had three miscarriages.

As always, he had a short-back-and-sides haircut and sported a small brown beard that had been kept clean and trim. As always, he was wearing a checked sports jacket and flannels. His shoes were a gleaming black, and his shirt white with a stiff collar held in place by a brass stud. The only item of clothing that ever seemed to vary was his tie, which, on this occasion, was dark blue with white dots instead of pure navy blue.

At well over six feet tall, powerfully built and with a military bearing, he cut an imposing figure and had undoubtedly excelled on the sports field.

Willard had sensed some time ago that, despite his apparent lack of logic, Aubrey Forsdyke was not a man to be trifled with.

"I can see that you don't believe me and I can, to some extent, understand your scepticism," Mr Forsdyke said. "I am sure that your previous attempts to catch my wife out were thorough and genuine... and I wouldn't dream of accusing you of incompetence!"

"Thank you!" Willard replied, tongue in cheek.

"…which is why I am asking you to work for me again!"

"It's your money!" Willard replied wearily.

Aubrey Forsdyke's blue eyes flashed and his cheeks reddened, but he managed to hang on to what remained of his composure. "I am now convinced, beyond a shadow of a doubt, that Estelle is up to something," he declared. His sonorous, cultured voice, a voice that would lend itself perfectly to a church sermon, contrasted starkly with Willard's slightly West Country burr that was delivered in a slightly higher pitch.

"Please tell me about it," Willard said, this time more attentively.

"She's been leaving the house more often, and she keeps making mysterious telephone calls," his client told him. "There have also been incoming calls. When I pick up the receiver, the caller has hung up. When Estelle is on the phone, she becomes all mysterious and she quickly hangs up when she sees me."

"That sounds strange. Do you have any idea where she goes, on leaving the house?"

"I didn't until a few days ago. Before that, it was a case of Estelle going shopping, or not being in the house when I return home from work."

"So what's happened now?"

Aubrey Forsdyke's massive chest swelled as he sighed. "She has been seen in the company of another man!" His sense of outrage could not have been more apparent.

"Do you know who the man is?"

"No, I don't, and he has only been seen from a distance."

"Who saw him, and where was he seen?"

"I heard about it from someone at my church, and she said she had seen the two of them together on three separate occasions."

"Whereabouts?"

"Always under the pier. Not the main pier, but the one that is no longer in use and people don't go to anymore."

"Did they embrace, or anything like that?"

"I don't know. They were only seen from a distance, and it has always been early in the evening… when it has started to grow dark and always before I was due to be back from work."

"Have you any idea at all who the man is, or, if not, what he looks like?"

Aubrey Forsdyke sighed again. "I have no idea who he is. All I know is that he is above-average height and youngish-looking… younger than my wife. He also looks vaguely thuggish, apparently, and that's something else that worries me."

For the first time, Willard was able to sound intrigued and mean it. "All right," he said. "I will look into this. Perhaps, in the meantime, you could give me your witness's name and contact details."

Visibility was poor as early as the late afternoon, when Willard selected a spot from where he could watch what comings and goings there might be around the redundant pier. Until recently, the area around it had become known as a haven for young lovers. However, it was now much more a magnet for drug dealers and their customers and few others frequented it.

The usual hubbub of activity on and around the main pier could be heard easily, although all that could be seen of that pier was an outline. Although just a short walk away, it was a different world than the one Willard had just entered.

He had picked a position halfway up a sloping path, from which he could sit behind a bush and look down on the redundant pier and the expanse of sand and pebbles that lay below it.

Just before the sky closed in completely and made watching anything impossible, two figures appeared below the pier. They belonged to a big man and a small man, who were engaged in a transaction of some sort. The small man handed over what looked like money and the big man gave him a parcel before the pair parted and walked away in separate directions.

Willard realised he would have to come back another day.

In the meantime, there was a Miss Ramirez to see.

After opening the post and leaving Cicely in charge the following morning, he made his way to what had become known as the 'Warsaw Region'. Occupying a parcel of land in the north-east of Bridgetown, it was known for its high proportion of immigrants, especially Poles and Italians. The cottage home of Miss Ramirez, a Mexican, was on the northern edge of the area and within three minutes' walk from the church frequented by Aubrey and Estelle Forsdyke.

Miss Ramirez, another regular at the church, was known as someone who had a knack for acquiring intimate knowledge of virtually every member of the congregation. Little was known about her, though, except that she had been abandoned as a baby at a police station, raised in an orphanage and had lived in Bridgetown for almost all her life.

"Estelle is not unfaithful to her husband, never has been and never will be," she told Willard as soon as he had sat down in her sparsely furnished sitting room.

Willard was immediately struck by her cut-glass accent and impeccable diction, but was not remotely surprised by what she had said.

Miss Ramirez was fifty-ish, above average height and slender. Her olive skin was devoid of wrinkles and her dark brown eyes had an air of sadness about them. She wore no make-up, was smartly but conservatively dressed, and appeared to be every bit as mysterious and remote as Willard had heard she was.

"I can see you got the expected answer," she said matter-of-factly.

Willard admitted this was the case, and said he was just doing his job.

"I appreciate that," Miss Ramirez said. "I know what Aubrey Forsdyke is like and I should imagine this is not the first time he has put you on a wild goose chase."

"You are quite right, and I can't help wondering why," said Willard. "However, it would be useful if you could tell me whether it's true that Estelle has been going out a lot lately and meeting a man under the derelict pier."

Miss Ramirez gave a dry chuckle. "It's not at all how it might look," she said "Aubrey Forsdyke is a very insecure man for a start. He began to woo Estelle almost as soon as she had left school. Estelle has always been a very shy person. She had repressive parents, who are now dead, and saw marriage to Aubrey as a means of escape from them."

"That sounds absolutely terrible, but it doesn't really explain her unusual recent movements."

Miss Ramirez's eyes displayed a rare flicker of emotion. "I am about to come to that," she said. "One of the reasons she has been away from her home lately is that she has often been here, where she can pour herself out and get some respite from an overbearing and possessive husband."

"I must admit that I don't find that hard to believe," Willard said. "What about the meetings under the pier, though?"

Miss Ramirez chuckled again. "Estelle has been acting as a go-between," she said.

"How do you mean?"

"She has been helping another member of the congregation at our church, a middle-aged lady, who's been having a tryst with a much younger man. The couple concerned both want the affair kept a secret, and Estelle is helping them by passing on notes about when, where and how they can meet. I don't really approve of what's going on. It goes against everything I have been taught and believe in… though I can sympathise in this case."

"Why's that?"

"The young man is a bit of a misfit, a bit of a thug, in fact. But he has emotional problems apparently, and the lady he is seeing seems able to help him. The lady is lonely and I know her well enough to know that, despite her prim exterior, she has quite a sex drive!"

"Good grief!" exclaimed Willard. "Who are these people? What on earth am I going to say to Mr Forsdyke?"

"That's up to you," said Miss Ramirez. "But you can see now that he has nothing to worry about. The people having a secret affair have nothing to do with your investigation. The lady concerned is a friend of mine and I am in no way prepared to give you her name."

"What about the young man she's seeing?" Willard had no need to know, but curiosity got the better of him.

Miss Ramirez waved a hand dismissively. "I hardly know him," she replied. "His name is Sebastian, I believe."

After Willard voiced thanks and left Miss Ramirez's cottage, he decided to pop into a coffee bar he happened to espy a hundred yards down the road. There was much to muse about, not least the question of what exactly to say to Aubrey Forsdyke.

As he sat near a window with a drink and a roll, he saw a young woman pass by and instinctively knew who she was. She was short, stocky and wearing a long-sleeved dress that even covered her ankles. Her auburn hair was in a bun and, Willard knew that, like Miss Ramirez, she wore no make-up. Her face was rosy and pretty and Willard knew that even the permanent forlornness of her expression did not detract from the prettiness. He watched as she approached the door to Miss Ramirez's cottage and went inside.

It looked very much like a closed case, though Willard felt duty-bound to conduct at least one more vigil near the pier.

So, later that day, he took up the same position as he had done the day before. Before long, he could see the figure of a young man appear from the right and pace up and down a bank of pebbles not far from the pier, but too far for Willard to get a good look at him. The young woman seen from the coffee bar window appeared from the opposite direction a few minutes later, and the pair converged on to a spot under the pier where they could be seen less easily.

The meeting lasted for a minute at the most. A few words were exchanged before the woman produced an envelope and the young man snatched it from her before walking away.

CHAPTER 9

"Where are my knickers?!" the new Advertising Manager asked again. It was three in the morning, and she was unable to suppress a giggle. Hubert and Shirley had been in the *Argus* boardroom since eight o'clock the previous evening, and Shirley was almost fully dressed. "You're a bit of a bastard, aren't you?!" she said in a tone that suggested anything but hate.

"And you're a bit of a tinker," replied Hubert, who then bent Shirley over a table, pulled up her skirt and slapped her bare buttocks three times before entering her once more.

"You can have your knickers back now," he declared, once he had finished. He pulled them out of a trouser pocket, opened Shirley's handbag and put them inside. "Time for me to take you home," he then said, before taking her arm and steering her towards the firm's car park.

During the short drive home, Hubert had just one hand on the wheel and Shirley loved the way the other hand was used to caress her. Shirley knew she was being used, if not abused, and was relishing every moment. The attention she was receiving was irresistible. Attention was something she had craved for a long time. Her marriage had been something of a nightmare. It had been devoid of anything approaching affection, and she had become accustomed to being treated with indifference, even disdain.

The salary Hubert had offered her if she joined the *Argus* had been tempting, too. It was almost half as much again as she had been getting at the *Bugle*, though her prime reason for moving was to be closer to her lover.

Hubert was in an upbeat frame of mind as well. The Bond Brothers, one of the smaller firms of estate agents in Bridgetown, had just decided to leave the agents' cartel and the *Bugle* and go back to advertising in the *Argus*. Hubert had got Kelvin Watson, the new Editor, to write a front-page piece about this 'important new development'. He was hopeful that the other agents would soon follow suit, especially as he now had their beloved Shirley 'Tinker' Bell on board, and he planned to spend a lot of time talking to them himself.

In addition, his redundancy programme was going according to plan, and further savings were made with some staff quitting voluntarily and not being replaced.

Lord Perryman had expressed delight on hearing that the estate agents looked set to support the *Argus* once more, though he was saddened to learn of the impending losses of 'those wonderful writers'.

Hubert also had the newspaper's latest circulation figures to hand, but decided to keep this detail to himself for the time being.

The first of the feature writers to go was the fashion specialist, Mildred Pitt, a lady with exquisite taste and perfect manners, who had been with the *Argus* from the day she left Oxford University with a First in English. Although widely regarded as rather too prim and intellectual to be a journalist, she had soon won respect from both colleagues and the public with her impeccable prose.

Now in her mid-fifties, she was looked up to more than ever by most of those she worked with. However, there were one or two who believed she was failing to keep up with the times. Most of Mildred's fashion advice was arguably aimed too much at women of her generation rather than youthful 'yuppies', who formed a significant part of the newspaper's readership.

The first to suggest to Hubert that Mildred might be past her sell-by date was Jane Smith. Hubert responded by patting her gently on a shoulder and bringing the subject up with Kelvin Watson and Andy McCallum.

"You need to make your copy shorter and you must aim it much more at a young audience," the Editor told the fashion guru the following day.

Mildred was visibly taken aback, partly because of his curt manner. "Has anyone complained?" she answered with an air of disbelief.

"Your copy is convoluted," said the Deputy Editor, who gave her a look that would have sunk a battleship. He was a man of few words, who had few friends and was feared by almost everybody.

"I am afraid that, whether you like it or not, there are going to have to be changes," Kelvin Watson then said. "We are going to have to do more for younger people, and the stories and articles in the *Argus* will have to be shorter and crisper."

Mildred had never felt so chastened as she returned to her desk. The fear of being under the cosh was foreign to her, and she had never felt so insecure. She suddenly found she had to reconsider her position, and she needed to do something quickly.

One of her first thoughts was to contact the up-and-coming glamour model Loretta Robey. She had met her briefly once before, did not get on with her particularly well and was far from impressed by the way she dressed. "Far too loud and in your face for my liking," was how she summed up her appraisal to curious colleagues. However, she did seem to represent everything that was youthful and modern, and Mildred hoped that an interview with Loretta would bring the right results.

Mildred looked for the telephone number that lay in the little black book that contained details of how all her contacts could be reached, and got in touch with Loretta's agent. "I'm sure something can be arranged," the agent told her. "We will get back to you soon."

As she put the receiver down, Mildred could sense that someone was standing behind her. It was Andy McCallum.

"How arr ye gitting on?" the Deputy Editor asked her. He was one of the few people she felt unable to look in the face, though she was well aware that she was being given the evil eye that seemed to be his trademark.

"I am arranging to interview Loretta Robey, the glamour model," she said.

McCallum stared at her for a few seconds, before saying, "Good!" and returning to his work station.

Once he had gone, Mildred fled to the ladies' cloakroom, sat in a cubicle and wept. After five minutes, she emerged from the cubicle, washed away the tears, adjusted her make-up and returned to her desk. As she struggled to regain her composure, her telephone rang and an interview with Loretta Robey was fixed.

As she put the receiver down, a messenger appeared with a bundle of copies of the latest edition of the *Argus*. As soon as Mildred received one, she thumbed through it until she reached the page devoted to the world of fashion and discovered that the latest article she had written was not there. Her piece had been devoted to the subject of fashion accessories through the ages and had involved a lot of research beforehand. The page was instead given over to the subject of miniskirts and how young women could display their legs to best advantage. There were lots of pictures and a minimum of words. No local writer or photographer had been involved in the work, and it was clear that the material was syndicated and had been garnered through a press agency.

"Well, what do you expect?!" McCallum said to her, as she sat with head in hands. He was standing behind her again. "You need to git yer finger out," he added with a snarl.

Most of Mildred's colleagues who were present to witness the incident felt a sense of relief that they were not the ones being singled out for this sort of treatment.

The notable exception was Hamish McLennan, who was seething with anger. "If there's one thing I can't stand, it's a bully!" he muttered.

"I'm looking forward to this interview," Loretta Robey declared with a cheeky grin.

Mildred felt ill at ease, and that she was being mocked. She had arrived at the photographic studio a few minutes before the agreed time and had what she felt was the dubious privilege of seeing her interviewee pose semi-naked. Loretta was particularly popular among men for the way she posed or paraded in swimwear, underwear or less, and it was not hard to see why. It was no coincidence that she had entered and won Miss Universe competitions in Britain and abroad.

Mildred experienced a sense of relief that she had at least had the grace to put on a dressing gown.

"It's very kind of you to see me," she said nervously.

Loretta grinned. Her interviewer's reputation had reached her already, and the glamour model had always had a sense of fun. "I understand you want to know what sort of clothes I wear," she said.

"Yes, I want to focus a bit more in the future on the tastes of younger people," Mildred replied.

"So you're looking for a change?"

"You could say that."

Loretta began to laugh. "Me, too!" she said. "Most people are only interested in me *not* wearing clothes!"

Mildred managed to see the funny side, too, and suggested to Loretta that she might like to be seen in a different light.

Loretta went to a large suitcase that was lying in a corner and said: "I have brought along a few examples of what I like when in cover-up mode!" The two women both smiled.

Most of the outfits Loretta produced were on the skimpy side and, in Mildred's mind, pretty tasteless. However, there was a twin set that made Loretta look almost refined and a trouser suit that Mildred would have happily worn herself.

The two women began to warm to each other and, once Loretta had shown Mildred the last item in the case – a long-sleeved mini-dress – she offered to make her interviewer a coffee, and the offer was readily accepted.

As they chatted over their drinks, Mildred discovered that they had more in common than most people might have guessed.

Loretta had been educated at Bridgetown's most highly regarded grammar school and had excelled in English. Had she not won so many beauty contests and not had an already burgeoning career as a model, she might well have gone to university. Another factor was that her family was hard up financially, and she was keen to help pay the bills.

"You're certainly not a bimbo!" an admiring Mildred commented.

Loretta chuckled. "I guess it's not hard to assume that all the girls in my line are so thick that they can't do anything else," she said. "Mind you, I have never tried very hard to allay that impression… not until now, anyway. Perhaps I should…"

The appearance of an *Argus* photographer made her stop in mid-sentence.

"I'd better go and change into something uncomfortable!" Loretta quipped.

"I guess I had better leave you to it," Mildred replied with a smile.

There were no smiles at the office, though. As soon as she got back, she was greeted with a snarl and a "Where have ye bin?" from Andy McCallum.

"I've been interviewing Loretta Robey, as I have already told you I was going to do," Mildred replied with a hint of irritation.

McCallum gave her his customary stare, before saying: "The Editor wants to see your copy as soon as it's finished."

Mildred's face reddened. "I will write it up as quickly as

I can, and it will be done a lot more quickly if there's no one breathing down my neck!" she retorted angrily.

The Deputy Editor walked away and Mildred got cracking with her latest project. "I'll show them!" she said to herself.

It took her just over half an hour to write a piece that was not just devoted to Loretta's somewhat limited fashion tastes, but also, and much more, to her personality and unseen intelligence. The writing style was as exquisite and impeccable as ever, and Mildred was convinced that her readers would be fascinated by the revelation that she was far from the bimbo she was possibly thought to be. The Editor ought to be impressed as well, she felt.

Kelvin Watson gave Mildred a stony look as she entered his office and told him she had finished her article. Andy McCallum was sitting with him. "Leave it with me," the Editor said.

A full two hours passed, and she heard nothing. Mildred was yet to have a break that day, so she popped out for a while to do a bit of shopping and, while doing so, give thought to what she should write about next. One possibility was another interview with Loretta, perhaps on something unrelated to fashion. It was, after all, good to diversify now and again.

By the time she had returned to work, she had decided to do this and reached for her telephone. Apart from anything else, she had enjoyed Loretta's company.

But, as she reached for her telephone, she sensed that McCallum was standing behind her yet again. And, on turning round, she could see that she was getting the usual evil eye.

"It's just another piece of convoluted crap, isn't it?!" he snarled. The snarl turned into a roar, when he added: "You need to get your fucking finger out!"

CHAPTER 10

"We've got another estate agent willing to advertise with us," Hubert told Lord Perryman on the telephone. "That's excellent!" the proprietor replied. "Is there any sign that the others might follow suit?" Hubert assured Lord Perryman that he was working hard on that, and would keep him posted.

"Nice one!" said Jane, who happened to be in Hubert's office at the time. Her skirt was shorter than ever, and she was eying her boss lasciviously. "Who have you got on board?" she asked.

"Johnny Simmons, the ex-footballer. He has decided to embark on a new career as an independent estate agent, and he is setting up shop on Monday week."

"Hmm, I wouldn't mind meeting him!" said Jane, who had seen photographs of him.

"I have no doubt that can be arranged!"

"Presumably he's not part of the agents' cartel?" Jane asked a little more seriously.

"You are quite right!" Hubert said with a smirk. "That's a detail I forgot all about."

"How are you getting on with the others?" Jane then asked.

"Pretty well," said Hubert. "Tinker Bell and I have been busy chatting them up, and I am optimistic. You can put in your diary that we're having a meeting with them all in the boardroom in three days' time."

"Would you like me to lay on some goodies?"

"Of course. And I want you to be there… and it would do no harm if you were wearing the skirt you have on now!"

Jane tittered. "Will Johnny Simmons be there?"

"I certainly hope so. And he will need to be impressed by what we have to offer, like all the others."

All the agents were there on the big day. So, too, were a local banker and a couple of council officials, along with Kelvin Watson, his secretary Pauline and Kirsty Kirkham, the newly appointed *Argus* Property Correspondent. Hubert Weaving and Shirley 'Tinker' Bell were on hand to greet the guests as they arrived, while Andy McCallum was left to hold the fort in the Editor's office.

With Hubert's approval, Jane had got Bridgetown's leading catering firm to bring along champagne, wine, sandwiches and an assortment of canapes and cakes.

Hubert and Kelvin had both donned their pinstripes, while Jane, Shirley, Kirsty and Pauline were all clad in figure-hugging trouser suits of identical design.

The drinks flowed freely, the food was consumed with alacrity and social interactions became increasingly convivial as the afternoon wore on and Hubert's charm offensive took hold.

Hubert and Shirley had, of course, done a lot of spade work in advance. They had told all the agents that the terms and level of service they could expect from the *Argus* in future would bear no comparison with what they had received before. The agents had been far from receptive to Hubert's initial approach, but the new Company Secretary was now convinced that he had now softened them up enough to, at least, discuss terms. One of the obvious attractions for the agents was that advertising with the *Argus* once more meant they could work with their beloved 'Tinker'.

Once Kelvin, Pauline, Kirsty, Jane, the banker and the two council dignitaries had departed, Hubert and Shirley directed the agents through a door to one side that led to a slightly smaller room, where they could all sit round a long table.

The agents continued to haggle over the cost of advertising in the *Argus*, though they had become more receptive and less strident in attitude. A number of proposals, some of them made before, were advanced by each side, and eventually an agreement was reached.

The agents were, as might be expected, all skilled negotiators, and they drove a hard bargain. In the end, the deal that was struck was the best that Hubert had hoped for.

For the first three months, the advertising rates would be so low that the *Argus* would initially be facing a slight loss. The rates would then rise to levels that would still be lower than they were before the agents switched from the *Argus* to the *Bugle*, but they would at least lead to a profit.

The agents had the option to pull out after three months if they were in any way dissatisfied with the service they were receiving, and the contract as a whole contained the condition that Shirley would be on hand at any time to tackle any problems that might arise. The problems could relate to the wording and design of advertisements, the use of pictures and all aspects of the production process. In addition, the new Property Correspondent was to provide 'good, informative editorial' to accompany the advertisements.

Everyone was wreathed in smiles when the meeting round the table came to a close. "It's a pleasure to do business with you," the leader of the cartel said to Hubert, with the warmest of handshakes, as the agents all left.

After seeing them out, Hubert and Shirley did a little jig around the boardroom.

"We've cracked it at last!" Hubert exclaimed triumphantly. "We're in business!" Shirley shouted, delighted to see her lover so happy. The pair then did a little more than a jig, before suddenly remembering that the caterers were due back any time to collect the crockery, cutlery and silver goblets they had loaned out.

Lord Perryman expressed delight when Hubert telephoned to tell him the news. When told about the terms, he was less delighted but prepared to accept the inevitable. "At least we've got them back! That's the main thing," he said. "Well done! And congratulations once more for getting Shirley Bell on board."

"It took a bit of doing, I have to say," said Hubert. "However, my life is a lot easier now that we've got her around."

After a short silence, Lord Perryman then said: "There are, of course, lessons to be learned from all this. One of those lessons is that we must not rely so heavily on just one sector of activity for advertising in the future. I have no doubt you are aware of that, and that there can't be any question of us resting on our laurels."

Hubert, who had sensed from early on that, in spite of his Bertie Wooster-like appearance and demeanour, the *Argus'* proprietor was far from a fool, assured him that the word complacency was not in his vocabulary.

"The next part of my strategy is to woo the Bridgetown business community," he then said. "Shirley and I plan to ensure that the local estate agents get a level of service that is second to none, and hold that up as an example of what we are about at the *Argus*. We are going to show everyone in the town that they have a new kind of newspaper, with a new Editor and a new dynamism. My next plan is to woo the business folk, whether they be bankers, insurance companies, building societies or merely shopkeepers or market traders."

"How do you plan to do the wooing?" Lord Perryman asked.

"It will involve a lot of personal contact and lots of legwork by my reps and, to some extent, by yours truly. I also plan to stage a series of events that people in the business community and members of the public can sometimes attend."

"Excellent! Do you have any specific events in mind?"

"I'm working on that right now. One of the first events I plan is an open-air fair-cum-market, at which all the local traders can have stalls. It could have the added attraction of someone famous being present to open the event, meet the traders and sign autographs."

"Do you have anyone in mind to do this… someone who is not too expensive?"

"Yes, I do," said Hubert. "One definite possibility is that local glamour model. Her name is Loretta Robey, I believe."

"That sounds brilliant," said Lord Perryman. "But won't you need to take on some helpers for that?"

"Yes, I have thought of that. I might need to appoint a new advertising executive, but, on the editorial side, I will get Kelvin to redeploy a couple of his reporters. One of them could be made Business Editor, and, in this case, there could be a modest pay rise."

Lord Perryman made it clear that he was impressed with what had been done and what was planned for the future, but not without reservation. "I have not done the mathematics, but does any of this mean you will be able to, at the very least, defer your redundancies programme?"

"I wish I could," said Hubert. "Unfortunately, the strategy I have devised is going to entail an initial outlay, and so the question of pruning of, if I dare call it, dead wood, has become more urgent, if anything. We don't yet know for sure what the estate agents will do after three months and, in the meantime, we are running at a loss with them."

The term 'dead wood' rankled with Lord Perryman, but the proprietor was able to contain his anger and admit that Hubert had a point.

"I can't help admitting that I am going to miss the work of those wonderful feature writers," he murmured. "I still can't get my head round the idea of there being an *Argus* with no Mildred Pitt, in particular."

CHAPTER 11

"I didn't know you were planning to stage a fete," Jane said to Hubert.

"Neither did I!" was the reply. "The idea came up while I was talking to dear old Perryman on the phone… it's what's known as thinking on your feet!"

"There's certainly plenty to think about now!" said Jane. "What are we going to do next? Or perhaps I should ask what I am going to do next!"

"You are absolutely right!" said Hubert. "This *is* a job for you! The first thing you can do is look into the question of where such an event can be held and what the cost is likely to be. You can also contact that glamour model, Loretta something or other, and see if she is willing to participate."

"I will get on to it straight away," Jane promised. Hubert could sense that the 'fantasy woman' of the *Bridgetown Argus* was becoming increasingly impressed with his masterful manner. "Good girl!" he said with a grin.

"There's just one more thing," Jane then said, after a pause. "Mr Finklater is still waiting to see you."

"Oh, yes," said Hubert. "...Let him wait a little longer."

Joseph Finklater had been standing in a nearby corridor for almost forty-five minutes, before Jane let it be known that her boss was ready to see him. He had just turned sixty, and arthritis was beginning to get the better of him.

The veteran book and theatre critic, who had worked at the *Argus* for thirty-one years, did not wait to ask if he could sit down. He simply grabbed a small wooden chair that lay near the door of Hubert's office, pulled it towards Hubert's desk and sat.

"What can I do for you?" Hubert asked him icily.

"It's about that early retirement package," Joseph said. Hubert could see that he looked at the end of his tether.

"And what have you decided?"

"I think I will take it."

"So you should! It's a very generous package, the best sort of package anyone could hope to get anywhere. You can pack up your personal belongings and depart this week, even today, if you wish. I will leave that up to you."

Joseph managed a weary "Great!" as he rose to his feet and walked towards the door.

"It is, isn't it?" said Hubert. "I wish you well in retirement. In the meantime, I have a lot of things to get on with. One of them is to sort out the journalists. It is high time they got off their arses and did some bloody work!"

Hubert was rubbing his hands with glee even before Joseph had left the room. Jane could see how upbeat he was, when he told her to sort out the necessary paperwork.

"Once that's been done, we can prepare a statement for dear old Perryman about where we are now and what our future financial projections look like," he said.

"Will do," said Jane. "I will have Finklater sorted in a trice."

"Well done!" said Hubert. "We could also have a chat about how we can go forward in the future. As you know, I value your input… which, of course, is reflected in your salary."

"That would be great!" Jane smiled broadly.

"I thought you might like that!"

Jane then asked Hubert if he had any more thoughts on the plan for a fete.

"Yes, I am going to get in touch with that Loretta something-or-other. She could be very useful to us, and I don't mean just the fete. If she's not too expensive, we could get her involved in other promotional activities."

"Would you like me to get in touch with her, to fix an appointment?"

"No, leave that to me," said Hubert. "It might be fun to chat her up a bit!"

"Fine," said Jane, who was now looking less pleased than a moment ago!

Hubert had reason to be displeased himself, when he learned a little later that Andy McCallum was off sick. Andy had come to the *Argus* with a reputation of having never taken a day off in his life. He was even known to be in the building, for reasons that were often not known, when he was supposed to be on holiday.

Hubert could not escape from the thought that there was some link between Andy being off sick with the sudden departure of Mildred Pitt. He was, after all, well aware of Andy's ability to hasten departures!

He decided to sound out the Editor, Kelvin Watson. Kelvin's lower lip quivered when he was asked what had happened to his Deputy. The normally blunt-talking Yorkshireman was unusually reticent.

"I believe he got involved in an argument," he said eventually.

"What sort of argument?"

"A violent one."

Hubert began to grow impatient. "Would you mind being a little more specific?" he said testily. "Who was the argument with, and who was being violent? And how? And why was there an argument at all?"

"I think it had something to do with Mildred," said Kelvin. "...and Hamish."

"How do you mean?"

"I believe that Hamish, who, as you have doubtless heard, has an explosive temper, was livid about the way Andy had treated Mildred."

"Really?!"

"By that, I mean Hamish has a tendency to be anti-establishment at times, and has views that don't always coincide with yours or mine."

"So, what happened?"

Kelvin, who realised he could be accused of prevaricating, needed a sharp intake of breath before answering. "Andy and I had been having a discussion about what story to lead with in the next edition, when Andy said he needed to go to the loo, and he went off to the downstairs gents. A couple of minutes later, I saw Hamish go in there and, at the time, thought nothing of it."

"Oh dear!" said Hubert. "I think I know what's coming next!"

"You are quite right, of course, but the situation is not so straightforward as it may seem and it's impossible to prove anything. Andy did not reappear for at least twenty minutes and, when he did, he said he had excruciating stomach pains and had to go home."

"Was he marked?"

"Oh no! That would lead to questions, wouldn't it?! If what happened is what I think happened, Hamish knew exactly what he was at."

"Presumably Andy gave no indication of what happened himself?"

"Absolutely none," said Kelvin. "I think he knew only too well what would happen if he did!"

Hubert paused for a moment, before saying: "This is not acceptable. It cannot be tolerated. I think that, at the very least, McLennan should be interrogated. If we can establish that he is guilty of what we suspect, he should be sacked on the spot."

Kelvin winced, and it was not hard to see why. "Hamish McLennan is an excellent reporter, the best we are ever likely to get, but he is very much his own man. Anyone who tries to push him around or rubs him up the wrong way probably has a death wish!"

Only a select few knew exactly happened in the gents' loo that day, although rumours were rife. Among the few was Willard Shakespeare, who was sitting at a corner table at the Rose and Crown a couple of days later with Hamish, Joseph and a security man called Reuben. Hamish and Joseph were poles apart in temperament, but were allies nonetheless, while for Reuben the pub was a second home. Willard was no stranger to the place either.

Reuben had been regaling the others with some of his tales of derring-do beyond enemy lines in Iraq and

Afghanistan. Some of the tales put forward had changed a little after every two or three pints.

Willard and the others waited patiently for Reuben to stop to get a round in, and learn about the subject they were actually there for.

"As you know, I don't usually subscribe to violence," the erudite, mild-mannered Joseph observed. "But, in this case, I might be prepared to make an exception. Is what I have heard really true?" An intrigued Willard saw Hamish's already dark visage blacken further.

"Yes, I'm afraid it is," Hamish said. "I don't know how much you have heard, but I might as well tell you the story in full."

"It won't go beyond these walls, of course," said Joseph.

"Of course! I'm assuming that!"

"Has it got something to do with the sudden departure of Mildred Pitt?"

Hamish's dark eyes flashed and his right hand became a fist. He was not a particularly big man, but, a bit like Willard, he was built like a box of coiled springs and, unlike Willard, possessed a short fuse.

"Yes, it was the way she was treated… especially by that bastard McCallum, who was cruel to her. As you know, Mildred is a highly talented writer who would be an asset to any newspaper anywhere. She gave long and loyal service to the *Argus*, and there is no way the treatment she received could be justified."

"That's very true," said Joseph. "I once saw Mildred flee the newsroom after having an altercation with that charming new Deputy Editor!"

"I saw that, too," said Hamish, who was seething at the thought. "I was so angry that I felt the need to go outside for a while and try to calm down. The trouble is that I then had to go to the loo… and who should be in there but McCallum!"

"Unfortunate timing!" said Reuben, who had re-joined the others by then and plonked four filled beer mugs onto the table.

"It was unfortunate for McCallum, that's for sure!"

"Sounds like you thumped him!" said Willard.

"Yes, but not straight away. I first suggested he had been a bit harsh in his handling of Mildred. He responded with a torrent of expletives and Gorbals speak and told me he was in a position to do what he liked and that I should mind my own bloody business."

"He's an absolute charmer, isn't he?!" quipped Joseph.

"I was absolutely livid," said Hamish, who had not been brought up in the Gorbals of Glasgow but the mean streets of Edinburgh.

"I pushed the bastard into one of the cubicles, closed the door and belted him lots of times in the ribs and balls and pushed his head down the lavatory pan. I did not hit him in the face, though. That would have led to questions being asked. I also left him in no doubt that if he told anyone, I would be after him again."

"It couldn't have happened to a nicer fella!" Reuben said with a chuckle.

"What amazes me is that the *Argus* would hire such a bloke, especially in a position of authority, in the first place," said Willard.

"You've got a point," said Hamish. "Perhaps I should have gone after the bloke who hired him!"

The quartet then sat in silence for a while, all wondering what drama would unfold next at the *Argus*.

At much the same time, Hubert Weaving was in his office, mulling over what should be done about the newspaper's formidable, talented and potentially dangerous Chief Reporter. He did, of course, want to get rid of him. But that was easier said than done.

Any thoughts along those lines had to be put on hold, however, because trouble was beginning to brew over the fate of another senior journalist. It was big trouble, and it was going to incur the wrath of Lord Perryman.

CHAPTER 12

Cicely put the receiver down hurriedly when Willard entered the office. Willard pretended not to notice, though he had become increasingly intrigued by her recent behaviour. Although still an immense asset to his little business, she had become erratic, excitable and furtive of late. Willard's natural sense of curiosity – which some would regard as nosiness – meant he had to get to the bottom of this.

"Good morning, Willard," Cicely said as she saw him. "How did you get on last night?"

Willard, who had, without much enthusiasm, been looking into a case of a husband's suspected infidelity, said he had drawn a blank so far.

"I have nothing to report either," Cicely then said.

"No contact from Forsdyke?"

"No, not even from him!"

"Thank God for that, anyway!" said Willard, who then went to the kettle in the corner and made some coffee.

Cicely declined the offer of a drink for herself and instead asked if it was all right for her to go out for a while. The request surprised Willard because she rarely wanted to leave the room, even to go to the cloakroom. Willard was, in fact, a believer in only being at work if there was work to do. "If there is a lot of work to do, stay until it is finished," he would argue. "If not, why be here?" He had, in the past, told Cicely to go home early when there was not much on, and she had insisted on staying. On one occasion, there had been a heavy workload, and Cicely had stayed in the office until midnight to make sure it was all done.

Cicely sensed that Willard was surprised and apologised for making such a request. Willard waved the apology aside and told her why he was surprised. "Of course, you can go out!" he said. "Take your time!"

Cicely rose to her feet, put on her coat and left immediately, with a "Much appreciated!" She added that she would not be unduly long.

Once she had gone, Willard wearily opened what little post there was and noted that there were no new messages. The coffee was welcome after the previous night's fruitless vigil. And, with the suspected philanderer almost certainly at work during the daytime, he felt tempted to try to catch up on his sleep where he was.

However, curiosity continued to get the better of him.

Once he had finished his drink, washed his coffee mug and put it away in a cupboard, he decided to pop out for a walk. He had no particular destination in mind, but had the idea that, during the course of a stroll, he might see Cicely somewhere and get some idea of what she was up to. There was also an outside chance of gaining a sighting of the suspected philanderer, should he leave his workplace for some reason. So, all in all, he felt the decision to go out, rather than wait for the telephone to ring, was justified!

A stroll along the sea front seemed as good an idea as any. Just before Willard got to the front, a few minutes later, he passed a small coffee bar. It was a place he often used for social reasons, to take a client to, or simply as somewhere he could ponder over a case, or life as a whole.

Inside were two familiar figures. One was Cicely, the other Estelle Forsdyke.

"Now I *must* know what's going on!" he said to himself.

He popped into a pub that was fifty feet away on the other side of the street and found a seat near a window. "You're early today!" the landlady said with a grin. "Is your latest case driving you to drink?!"

"No, I'm here to make sure that your beer is up to scratch!" Willard replied. "That's the case I'm on just now!" The cheery landlady chuckled and disappeared.

He was just six sips into his pint, when he saw the two women emerge from the coffee bar and walk hurriedly together in the direction of the front. They crossed the road and passed within feet of the pub, and Willard sensed that, although there was no obvious indication, Cicely had seen him. His sense of logic told him that the most prudent and diplomatic step to take next was to go back to his office and not be involved. However, curiosity consumed him and logic had to take a back seat.

He watched Cicely and Estelle take a turning to the right and walk purposefully together away from the most populous part of Bridgetown, and began to follow from what he thought was a respectful distance. There was no doubt in his mind as to where they were going.

Willard made for the spot he had used before, to watch what was going on near the derelict pier. A young man was standing beneath it.

Willard cursed quietly at his failure to bring with him his binoculars, though he was almost certain it was the man who Estelle had met during the vigil that husband Aubrey Forsdyke had got him to make. He could see the two women walking towards him.

As they drew near, Cicely ran ahead and threw herself into the young man's arms. The pair embraced passionately and any doubts that they were anything but lovers were dispelled when Willard saw what Cicely was doing with one hand. "Good grief!" he said to himself. "The prim and proper Cicely's got herself a toy boy!" He guessed that he was less than half her age.

The 'prim and proper' Cicely must have also had a sixth sense, as she suddenly disengaged from her embrace and looked in Willard's direction. Willard knew that she would not have actually seen him, as he was camouflaged behind a tree, but realised nonetheless that she was being watched. Willard saw the pair talk briefly before they kissed quickly and walked away in separate directions. By then, Estelle had disappeared, and Willard realised that was what he should do, too.

After returning to his office, the uneasy thought that Cicely might not come back crossed his mind. Willard began to wonder how he would cope without her secretarial and practical nous. After half an hour, his door flew open and his heart soared. Then he saw who it was.

"Did you get my telephone message?" Aubrey Forsdyke demanded as his bulky form almost filled the doorway.

"No, I'm sorry," Willard replied, half mumbling. "I've been ultra-busy and haven't got round to checking messages."

The new arrival plonked himself down on to a chair opposite Willard's desk and said, "Never mind. I just wanted to let you know that I might well have some more work to put your way. Will you be available?"

Willard confirmed, with as much enthusiasm as he could muster, that he almost certainly would be, and his visitor departed.

I hope he doesn't think his wife is seeing me! Willard suddenly thought. *I would hate to incur his wrath!*

Thoughts along those lines were still lingering twenty minutes later, when Cicely reappeared. She walked to her desk, and began to place the few belongings that lay on it and in it into a plastic bag. Willard could see that she was blushing.

"What are you doing?" he asked needlessly. "Are you all right?"

"I'm leaving," she replied.

"Why?"

"I think you know perfectly well why!" Cicely's face was now scarlet. "I think it's for the best if I go straight away."

"Please stay. I don't want you to lose you. It's important to me that you stay. You can talk to me about anything, in confidence, if there's anything you are unhappy about, and I will do anything I can to help if you need it. I'm your friend."

"Then why did you fucking well spy on me?!"

Willard was genuinely taken aback. He had never seen her angry before, and had never imagined she was capable of swearing. "I'm sorry," he said. "Really sorry. My natural nosiness got the better of me, and it shouldn't have. All I want to be is your friend."

Cicely, who had not believed she could swear either, looked into Willard's eyes and then, without warning, burst into tears and sobbed uncontrollably for a full minute.

Willard waited for the sobbing to subside before saying soothingly: "Why not tell me all about it? Whatever you say will not go beyond these walls, I promise you. There's no need for you to bottle things up. You can trust me as a friend and, who knows, I might even be able to be of help to you."

The tears stopped and Cicely said she would think about it. Willard suggested she took the rest of the day off, and Cicely agreed. Once she had gone, Willard turned his mind to the case he had in hand and thought about the evening vigil that lay before him. In the meantime, there was little else to do apart from try to recall where some of his paperwork was. "Come back, Cicely… please!" he said aloud.

His prayers were answered the following morning. A slightly bleary-eyed Willard, having spent a tedious and fruitless night following the movements of a suspected philanderer, arrived at just before ten.

Cicely was there waiting for him. "It's just as well you trusted me with a key!" she said with a faint smile. Her composure had returned, along with her perceived persona, and her appearance offered no hint of a reaction to what had occurred the previous day.

"It's great to see you back," Willard said with feeling, "…and I apologise if you have been kept hanging around."

Cicely responded by putting on the kettle.

"I know what you must be thinking," she said eventually. "What is an old maid like me doing with a young man who's not even half my age?" Willard was unable to deny that observation, and Cicely was anything but surprised.

"The reason that I never married was that I spent a lot of my life looking after my illness-stricken parents, who needed day and night care," she went on. "I received very little help in this respect and my social life, for a large part of my life, was non-existent."

"Are your parents still alive?"

"No, they're both dead now. They died within a year of each other, with my mother passing away just over six months ago."

"That must have left quite a void for you," Willard said with a sympathetic noise.

"It certainly did, and I had to take steps to fill it. One of those was to became active with the church, which was where I first met Estelle Forsdyke. Another was to come and work for you. I have read lots of detective novels over the years, and had often wondered what it would be like to become a detective myself. That might explain why I was so keen to work with you, at a low rate of pay, in the first place."

"Well, at least you're in the right place! And you probably know more about Aubrey Forsdyke than I do?!"

"Yes, I think I do! I have got to know Estelle pretty well, and heard plenty about that husband of hers. Basically, he is a very insecure man. And he's insanely jealous, to the point of being repressive. He does not like Estelle being out of his sight, if he can help it, and he only seems to be happy about her when she's engaged in work of the church."

"Does he have any reason at all to believe she's been unfaithful?"

"None whatsoever. Estelle is a shy person, who has had a strictly religious upbringing and, for her, marriage absolutely embraces the vow of forsaking all others. She has confided in me a number of times about how jealous her husband can be and how much that upsets her. There is no doubt in my mind that she is beyond reproach."

"You must have got to know quite a few people at the church," Willard then said. The slight change in tack was entirely intentional.

Cicely reacted with a sigh. "It's not hard to see how *your* mind works, is it?!" she said.

Willard apologised and conceded that what she did outside office hours was none of his business. She did not, of course, have to tell him anything. However, he then added: "If you feel the need to talk about it, or anything else, for that matter, I can promise you that it will be strictly between you and me."

Cicely offered a wry smile, and admitted that her tryst with 'such a young man', was 'bound to arouse curiosity'. Willard kept his counsel as he waited for Cicely to elaborate.

"I met Sebastian… that's his name… through my work with the church," she said. "Estelle and I both help with a project that the vicar initiated to help young offenders who are on probation. A serial car thief was assigned to Estelle. I got Sebastian."

"What was Sebastian on probation for?"

"Acts of violence, mainly. He was always getting into arguments that turned into fights, largely because he had difficulty expressing himself. He did, and still does, badly lack self-confidence. One of my tasks, as I see it, is to build up his confidence."

"So, when someone upsets or goads him, he just lashes out?"

"Yes, that's about it," said Cicely. "…or so it seemed. At first, I wondered, not without trepidation, what I was getting into. As you can imagine, I was pretty nervous just before the first time we met."

"What was he like when you met?"

"Highly suspicious! He didn't seem to trust anyone. It was quite a job getting him to open up. However, after a while, I could sense that he was coming round to the idea that I was there to try and help him, rather than harm him. It soon became apparent that he totally lacked self-esteem, and that my main task was to try to build up his confidence."

"I have a feeling you succeeded."

"I would like to think so. Over a period, he became less aggressive outwardly and he became better at expressing himself."

"So you managed to establish a rapport?"

"Yes, we did. He would say, after a time, that he always looked forward to our meetings, which, initially, were just once or perhaps twice a week, and I began to look forward to those meetings as well. I felt I was doing something really worthwhile and that a new chapter in my life was beginning."

"Sounds like quite a chapter!"

Cicely began to blush, and her voiced quivered as she said: "He had his needs… and, believe it or not, so did I!"

Willard quickly realised a slight change of tack was called for. "Do you know why this young man, er, Sebastian, had problems in the first place?" he asked.

Cicely was visibly relieved. "I don't know all the answers to that, but one thing I do know is that he comes from a very unhappy home," she said. "His parents were oppressive and always feuding, and there is a particularly unpleasant older brother apparently. Sebastian is afraid of him, and I shudder to think what would happen if he found out about our relationship."

CHAPTER 13

Strong arms were his only asset when it came to swimming. His style was so tortuous that no ordinary man could employ it and complete more than three or four lengths of the local pool. With each overarm stroke, Brian Howes would roll from one side to the other with his head in the air and his legs akimbo. He was almost glacially slow, but, unlike any ordinary man, he was capable of racking up thirty laps.

Brian was a fitness fanatic who liked to engage in at least one physical activity every day. Thursday was his swimming day. On other days, he would run, walk, cycle, play tennis or football and work out with weights. He belonged to the Long-Distance Walkers' Association, had run two London Marathons in three and a quarter hours while in his early fifties and indulged in other sporting disciplines with varying degrees of success.

Most important to him was the need to do something every day. He was not entirely sure why this was so important, though; if he had stopped to think about it, he might have better recognised the need to drive out demons. As it was, he relied on medication as well as exercise.

Brian was going through a particularly hard time at the moment. His relationship with his domineering wife, Leslie, could be fraught at the best of times, but was particularly so at present as the couple had just learned that their son was in a gay relationship. And they could not agree on how to come to terms with the fact or how best to deal with the son.

Not surprisingly, Brian was feeling insecure at work, too. Recent departures, especially those of long-serving colleagues who had become friends, disconcerted him. He missed Mildred, in particular, and dreaded the thought that the axe could fall on him next.

He did not get on with the new Editor and Deputy Editor, and neither of them had said anything to allay his fears.

The blunt-talking Kelvin had let it be known that he liked to be addressed by his Christian name, that he liked copy to be short and sweet and that he disliked convoluted 'ego trips' as vehemently as alcohol. He favoured encouraging the young and had little time for journalists who were beyond their sell-by date. Brian suspected that, by now, he had been put in the 'past it' category. Meanwhile, Andy, who confirmed that he liked his Christian name to be used as soon as he heard Kelvin did… and developed a sudden dislike of beer… did not seem to like anyone or anything.

One of Brian's many worries was the way the new Editor was doing away with articles written for many years by *Argus* feature writers and replacing them with material bought in from press agencies. Such material would lack local flavour and be useable in newspapers throughout the country, even abroad. Its virtue, if it could be called that, was that column inches could be filled without having to employ local journalists to fill them.

Brian's main claim to fame was his ability to write vividly about walking and wildlife, though he could also turn his hand at handling news and sports stories if needed. He knew all the best walks, for walkers of all abilities, in the area and beyond, and his knowledge of local flora and fauna was widely respected.

Perhaps his most famed regular column was his weekly 'Howes That for a Walk?' It had impressed the previous Editor and the one before that, but the blunt and forthright Kelvin Ward rarely seemed to be impressed with anything.

Brian strained every sinew to make his walking column as near perfect as possible. He even tried to make it crisper, more succinct in his quest for approval.

His latest offering focussed on an area fifteen miles to the north of Bridgetown that was noted for its wood, waterfalls, rare birds and the occasional sighting of a red squirrel. At the Editor's behest, he filed his copy and submitted his latest, always modest, expenses claim.

As he did so, he had palpitations and began to hyperventilate. He had a premonition that something terrible was about to happen as a result of a perceived sin. He did not know what the sin was and, as his innate sense of guilt began to manifest itself, he tried to work out what he had done wrong. When he found he was unable to, he considered asking one or two colleagues what they thought. He knew that they knew he possessed a tortured soul. Mildred and Joseph were no longer around to be confided in, but there was always the irascible Hamish, who, despite his violent temper, had a kindly streak.

"You look as if you have a wee problem," Hamish said. "Take a pew and tell me about it." Hamish had no real knowledge or understanding of Brian's demons, but he was, at least, a good listener.

Brian faltered as he tried to work out where to start. Before he could, he was summoned to see the Editor.

"I have been looking at your expenses claim," Kelvin Ward told him, without inviting him to sit. "As you know, the firm has been having financial problems lately... and I am having to keep tabs on people who try to pull a fast one."

"What do you mean?" a spluttering Brian asked. Brian, a deeply religious man, was known throughout the building for his honesty as much as he was for eccentricity.

"The form you filled in is now with the Company Secretary," said Kelvin. "He wants to talk to you about it."

Brian's head began to spin, and he could sense there was no point in asking what the problem was. So he made his way upstairs and knocked on the Company Secretary's door.

"If you wait outside, Mr Weaving will see you shortly," Jane Smith told him. The firm's 'fantasy woman' was wearing a shorter skirt than ever.

The fact that he had to wait outside for a good half an hour did not surprise Brian in the least. Hubert Weaving's reputation for keeping staff – especially journalists – waiting had, by now, become established. Being aware of such a fact did nothing to allay his fears, though.

The palpitations returned and beads of sweat appeared on his brow as he tried to work out what he had done wrong. All he felt he knew was that the offence he had committed must have been the most heinous possible.

"You can go in now," Jane Smith eventually told him. She did so with a predatory smile that unnerved him even further.

Brian tentatively tapped on the Company Secretary's door twice and entered on hearing the command, "Come!" Once inside, he was told he 'had better sit down'. Hubert Weaving was holding up a piece of paper that Brian guessed carried his expenses claim. A pair of dark, boring eyes made him squirm, though he was yet to learn what there was to squirm about.

"I have been studying your latest expenses statement," Hubert said after a few seconds. "It makes for interesting reading."

All Brian could think of saying was, "Oh!"

Hubert echoed the "Oh!" and then, with eyes fixed firmly on Brian's eyes, asked: "Is that all you can say?"

"I don't know. What's all this about?" Brian's head was spinning, and he feared he was on the verge of a panic attack.

"It's about *this*!" Hubert said with a snarl, as he gave the piece of paper he was holding a slap. "Do you understand?"

"No, I don't. I don't understand at all!" Brian's normally high-pitched voice had become a quavering falsetto.

Hubert leaned forward and waved the piece of paper a few inches in front of Brian's face. The expenses claim consisted of three items: petrol, telephone calls and hospitality.

"The cost of petrol from Bridgetown to Snaresbury, where you say you started your walk, and back is a pound less than what you have said it was. I have worked it out by calculating the total mileage and using the company's mileage allowance rate. What do you have to say for yourself?"

"I'm sorry. I must have miscalculated."

"You *miscalculated*!" Hubert's lip curled, before he then said: "All right, I will let that one go… for the moment."

Brian was now in no doubt that there was more to come before the inquisition ended.

"I will also let go what you say about phone calls," Hubert added. "I will have to be charitable, I suppose, and assume you really *did* need to make them."

Brian felt relieved because he could not recall who he had made them to.

"Now we come to the cruncher!" said Hubert. "The question of hospitality."

Brian felt a sense of nausea overcome him as he racked his brains in an attempt to recall what he had written down.

"What sort of hospitality did you indulge in?" he was asked.

"I bought my contact a glass of beer," Brian said hurriedly.

"What, for *ten pounds*?!" Hubert roared. "Since when has a glass of beer cost *ten pounds*?!"

"I don't know. I must have made a mistake."

Hubert sneeringly echoed Brian's words: "You made a *mistake*! Rather an expensive mistake, don't you think?"

Brian's head continued to spin. He was unable to look his inquisitor in the eye. "Oh dear! It is rather a lot, isn't it?" he said pathetically.

"So, you accept that a claim of ten pounds for a glass of beer is excessive?"

Brian greeted the rhetorical question with a nod.

Hubert stared long and hard into his eyes. "What do you think we should do about it?" he asked after a couple of seconds.

Brian, whose only thought at that point was to flee from the Company Secretary's office as soon as he could, answered:

"I suppose you need to do what you see fit."

His state of mind was such that he would have even confessed to a murder he did not commit. As it was, he had come to the conclusion that he had committed an offence far more serious than he had ever imagined he could make. Brian braced himself for the news that the £10 in his claim would be disallowed and the possibility of a written warning.

That was not what Hubert had in mind, though.

Expressions of disbelief could be heard throughout the building the following day. Jane had pinned a notice onto every board she could find and, for once, she was not what everyone chose to be looking at. The wording of the notice stunned everyone, especially those who knew Brian Howes even slightly.

"There must be some mistake!" one of the reporters said. "Brian Howes, of all people! He's the most honest person at the *Argus*."

"Or anywhere else, for that matter!" another added.

Yet there it was. The Company Secretary's notice made it abundantly clear that Brian had been sacked because of irregularities over expenses, and that anyone else who was found guilty of such an act, or any other form of fraud or dishonesty, could expect the same treatment.

During the course of the day, the feeling of disbelief turned into one of anger. The fact that Brian Howes had mental health issues was known to several colleagues already, and the decision to sack him made them livid.

Unofficial representatives from every department got together for talks, and it was decided to hold a meeting at which every staff member in the building could attend. Its prime purpose would be to discuss ways of helping and supporting Brian. The other aim would be to see if anything could be done about the new Company Secretary... who, by now, was universally referred to as 'The Vulcan'.

Meanwhile, the sight of Hamish McLennan shadow boxing behind a van in the car park came as no surprise to anyone.

The meeting was presided over by 'Big Al' Wright, a burly machine minder, who was known to be ever mindful of the need to protect his workmates from injustice. The welfare of journalists did not generally concern him, but this time it was different. He declared that 'The Vulcan' was a potential threat to every worker of every kind in the building, and urged everyone to attend.

Almost all of the sixty-four staff members whose presence was requested turned up. Apart from Hubert Weaving, Shirley Bell, Kelvin Ward, Andy McCallum and Jane Smith, the only people who did not appear were a couple of accounts clerks and a deaf tea lady who did not know what was happening.

'Big Al' opened the meeting by declaring that it was an historic occasion for the staff at the *Argus* because every department was represented, and stressing the importance of safeguarding the livelihoods of everyone. He then talked about how 'The Vulcan' had seen fit to sack a long-serving colleague, and contended that he should not be allowed to get away with it.

"Has anyone here been in touch with Brian since he left?" he then asked.

"I've been on the phone to his wife," said Hamish. "She was quite hysterical, and it sounds from what she said that Brian has had a nervous breakdown." The irascible Chief

Reporter was unable to conceal his rage. "I plan to call her later, and will keep you updated."

'Big Al' thanked Hamish for the information, before asking for views on what should be done. Hamish made mention of Brian's mental health issues, and this was confirmed by three other journalists.

"Does 'The Vulcan', or perhaps I should say Mr Weaving, know about this?" asked 'Big Al'.

"Does he care?" a van driver angrily asked.

"He obviously bloody doesn't!" Hamish roared. The rest of the room roared with him.

'Big Al' waited for the meeting to quieten down before asking if anyone would care to make a proposal on what should be done. One of the reporters suggested that he and two others should meet Weaving and see if he was prepared to reverse his ruling. The proposal was seconded and, after much discussion and the uttering of various expletives, this course of action was agreed and the meeting was closed.

As everyone began to disperse, Hamish turned to the person closest to him and said what a lot of people were thinking already: "There's not a cat in hell's chance of the bugger agreeing… and there will then be an all-out strike!"

CHAPTER 14

News of the strike at the *Argus* reached Lord Perryman at the very moment he was set to tee off at the 17th hole of his favourite course. Word reached him shortly after the club house telephone rang and the barman was ordered to let His Lordship know immediately.

"The caller demanded that you should know about it straight away," a breathless course maintenance worker, who had run up to him and given him the news, told him.

"How do you know there's a strike on?" Lord Perryman asked irritably.

"That's what the barman, who could not leave his post, told me," the maintenance worker said. "He asked the caller to leave a message because he knew you wouldn't want to be disturbed, but the caller said there was a strike on and that you had to be told straight away."

Lord Perryman hurled the iron he was about to hit a ball with at a small, recently planted sapling that almost snapped into two, and cursed. "I'm on my way!" he said.

A couple of hours later, he was on the road to Bridgetown. His chauffer had been summoned and told to drop anything else he might be doing. His ever-efficient young wife had packed a suitcase with everything he might need. Two hotel rooms at Bridgetown had been booked, too, in case they were needed.

Lord Perryman was still fuming. Having a game of golf cut short was bad enough. Having to deal with unrest at the *Argus* was beyond the pale. His love of newspapers and for the journalists who worked on them was matched only by his hatred of hassle. To make matters worse, the traffic that day was exceptionally heavy and there were numerous hold-ups. By the time his Rolls-Royce reached the *Argus* building, his frame of mind was little short of incendiary.

His entry to the company car park was blocked by around twenty strikers, some of them carrying placards. Lord Perryman got out of his Rolls and walked over to 'Big Al', who was at the forefront. The two men recognised each other.

"What's all this about?" Lord Perryman asked as calmly as he could.

'Big Al' outlined what had occurred and added that Mr Weaving had rejected calls for a meeting with staff.

"He flatly refused," said Hamish McLennan, who suddenly loomed up from behind.

"Where is Mr Weaving now?"

"Cocooned in his office, I should imagine," Hamish said angrily.

"Perhaps someone could show me where it is?"

"I'll do that," said 'Big Al', who had a feeling that Hamish and 'The Vulcan' should be kept apart for the moment.

Everywhere was eerily quiet inside. At first, there was not a soul to be seen. But, as Lord Perryman and 'Big Al' approached the Company Secretary's office, they could see Shirley Bell sitting forlornly in one corner and Jane Smith putting on nail varnish in another.

Voices could be heard from behind Hubert Weaving's door. "I'll leave you to it," said 'Big Al', who then departed.

Lord Perryman threw Hubert Weaving's door open without bothering to knock. Hubert was in there, having seemingly urgent talks with Kelvin Ward and Andy McCallum. The three men were clearly startled by the unexpected arrival.

"Perhaps you would kindly tell me what is going on?!" Lord Perryman rasped. The usual urbane preamble was conspicuous by its absence.

"We're having a discussion on what action we should be taking next," the Editor said weakly.

"I should bloody well think you are!" the proprietor roared. "Action is most definitely needed, and it needs to be taken yesterday! Have you, by any chance, reached a decision of some sort?"

"Not yet, I'm afraid," said Hubert. "The situation we're in is a tricky one."

"It seems to me that it's one of your own making!" Lord Perryman was struggling to contain his fury.

"That's not fair, sir," Hubert protested. "A member of staff has committed fraud, and I had no option but to sack him. What else was I supposed to do?"

"You could have behaved less like a Nazi!" Lord Perryman bellowed. "Ever since you came to the *Argus*, morale has gone down the toilet! Nobody wants to work here anymore, the quality of the paper has gone down, as has the circulation, and the whole damned situation has become a public talking point! At the rate things are going, the entire bloody business will go to the wall!"

"I thought the reason you hired me was to cut costs," Hubert retorted. He was beginning to grow angry himself, as well as flustered. "Are you saying I was wrong to sack Howes?"

"Yes, I am! Only a small sum of money was involved, and a written warning would have sufficed."

"So what do we do now?" asked Kelvin. "Are you saying we should now reverse our decision?"

"That would show weakness," said Andy.

Lord Perryman eyed the Deputy Editor and, with withering contempt, said: "It's good to know you are able to talk!"

"So what are we to do?" asked Hubert.

Lord Perryman took a deep breath, before saying: "I want the sacking of Brian Howes to be overturned. I don't care how you do it. If it makes you feel less *weak*, you can turn the sacking into a suspension. Once you've done that, you will need to take steps to boost the morale of the staff here and, at the same time, improve the paper's image. The *Bridgetown Argus* has always been seen as an important part of the community here, and it is vital that it stays that way."

Andy McCallum responded by leaving the room. "I need the toilet," he mumbled.

Hubert Weaving and Kelvin Ward, who were both visibly chastened, tried to gather their thoughts. "What can we do to bolster morale?" the latter eventually asked.

"Good question!" said Lord Perryman. "One thing I can do while I'm here is to make a point of talking to every member of staff. We can also have a reception for them with cheese and wine in the boardroom." He looked Hubert in the eye, before asking, with a hint of contempt: "Do you think you could manage that? You could get your assistant, the one who likes to flaunt herself, to organise it."

Hubert nervously agreed to 'get on to it'.

"We could have a fund-raising charity drive, perhaps to help the homeless, that the public could be involved in." The proprietor added: "A reception for the town's estate agents wouldn't be such a bad idea either. You could get your new Advertising Manager to organise that. I hope you are treating her well, by the way. She wasn't looking particularly happy when I saw her a moment ago."

"She's fine," said Hubert, whose only wish at that moment was for Perryman to get off his back. "I will have a chat with her about it."

"Isn't all this going to cost money?" Kelvin then asked.

Lord Perryman dismissed such a thought and said: "Good! Now, you have got a lot to get on with, haven't you?! The first thing you need to do is turn that sacking into a suspension, which can be quietly lifted later, and then get that reception for the staff organised. The reception can take place tomorrow, and I will be here to meet everyone."

"I will get onto these things, pronto," said Hubert, who reached for a telephone and dialled the number that he had been told 'Big Al' could usually be found on. The idea of facing pickets, especially when they included the fiery McLennan, did not appeal at the time. Relieved to hear the sound of the unofficial shop steward's familiar gravelly voice, he told him of the decision that would effectively give Brian Howes his job back.

"That sounds like good news!" was the response. "I will relay what you have said to my colleagues and get back to you."

A meeting of all the staff was arranged immediately, and a return to work the next day was agreed unanimously.

The chance to meet the proprietor and enjoy free refreshments did much to soften the mood of the staff. There were, of course, a few sceptics who said 'The Vulcan' was only organising the event because he had to, but, by and large, the frame of mind was positive. The return of Brian Howes, who was eccentric but well liked, was looked forward to, and many were curious to know what Lord Perryman was really like. And an added attraction for many of the males was the chance to ogle their 'fantasy woman' from close range.

Jane Smith was there in all her glory, wearing the skimpiest dress in her wardrobe. She was standing by the boardroom door to welcome arrivals, introduce them to Lord Perryman and ensure that they knew where the refreshments were. Hubert Weaving, Shirley Bell and Kelvin Ward helped with the hosting, while Andy McCallum sat in the newsroom below and handled incoming telephone calls.

After a while, Hubert and Shirley slipped away. However, Lord Perryman and Kelvin Ward remained to say at least one sentence to every individual in the room, while Jane continued to add decorative value.

After just under an hour, Lord Perryman delivered a short address, in which he emphasised how much he respected the *Bridgetown Argus* and everyone who worked on it. He concluded by saying that there were 'great plans for the future' and then handing over to the Editor to tell them a bit about what they were.

Kelvin Ward gave an address on how important the *Argus* was to the local community, and made mention of the planned charity drive to help the homeless and the reception for the agents. "These will be just for starters," he added. "Lord Perryman and I will, of course, be glad to hear of any ideas you might have... as valued members of our organisation... that could be of benefit to the newspaper."

However, everyone in the room was in for a shock.

As Kelvin began to emphasise how much the members of staff were valued at the *Argus*, Andy McCallum burst in and half-screamed at him: "Ye'd better come wi' me! I have some terrible news!"

"Bloody hell!" said Kelvin. "Is it really so bad that I can't even finish my bloody speech?!"

"Yes, it bloody is!" said Andy. "Brian Howes has gone and slashed his wrists! He's dead!"

CHAPTER 15

"You have really excelled yourself, haven't you?!" Lord Perryman said to Hubert, in the sort of withering tone that only an aristocrat seems able to accomplish.

He had burst into Hubert's office, without warning, to tell him the news that no one wanted to hear. Shirley was in the room at the time, and if the proprietor had not been in such a state of fury, he would have seen she had been crying. Shirley left as soon as he entered, and Lord Perryman picked up Hubert's telephone.

"Put me through to Nick Hemsley... at once!" he told the operator. The MD had left a number on which he said he could be contacted at all times. After a long pause, the operator said Mr Hemsley was 'unavailable until further notice'.

Lord Perryman slammed down the receiver, leaving Hubert guessing at what he wanted to talk to Hemsley about. "You had better go and see the widow!" he rasped. "You can tell her that the *Argus* will cover the cost of the funeral, and you can ask her if the company can help her in any other way.

Perhaps you can also find it in your heart… or what passes for one… to express condolences."

Hubert suggested it might be better to send someone else to carry out that task, but was told angrily: "No, I want you to do it yourself! If you find that difficult, it's too bloody bad!"

"All right, I will do it today."

"You will do it *now*!" Lord Perryman roared. "Once you have done that, you can get cracking on the project we are doing for the homeless. And you've got those estate agents to see as well, haven't you?!"

Lord Perryman stormed out of the room and out of the building and went to the Rolls-Royce that was just outside. The chauffeur was standing nearby, waiting.

The homeward journey was less fraught than the one he had taken to get to Bridgetown, but there was still plenty of time for him to think about what might have been.

He had inherited the *Argus* from his late, great father, a man he hardly knew. Like his father, he had been packed off to Eton as a boarder at an early age, but, unlike him, had yet to leave his mark on society. Lord Perryman senior had excelled in business, sport, academia and virtually every other field of endeavour and, for many years, been a highly respected politician and lecturer. The pinnacle of his fame came when he was appointed Under-Secretary at the Ministry of Defence, a post he held for almost a decade.

The current Lord Perryman was slightly above average at almost everything, but he had failed to stand out at anything. His desire to earn recognition from the public in general and his father in particular had become an obsession.

The answer had seemed to lie with the *Bridgetown Argus*, a tool he could use to exert influence and earn accolades. Recent events had done nothing to enhance his aspirations, and only his love of the English language and his fascination with journalism and journalists prevented him from considering putting the *Argus* up for sale. The sense of frustration that he had invested so much money in talented writers, and had now had to let some of them go, rankled as much as anything.

One of his greatest regrets had been the appointment of Hubert Weaving as Company Secretary, the man with the new broom, and he now wondered how best he could be rid of him.

Meanwhile, Hubert had fences to mend. He did not relish the prospect of a face-to-face meeting with Mrs Howes, but realised that there was no way out. He decided to get the task out of the way as quickly as possible, and then call in on the homelessness charity, which happened to be conveniently close. Time permitting, he could follow this up by introducing himself to some of the leading members of Bridgetown's business community. He could also look up Loretta.

Before leaving the building, he popped into the Advertising Manager's office and reminded Shirley of the need to start organising the estate agents' reception.

"When will I next be seeing you?" Shirley asked. Hubert gave her a grope that made her face redden and told her it would be soon.

By the time he reached the home of the late Brian Howes, he had his speech of sympathy worked out. Brian's wife, Cheryl, opened the front door and glared at him. She was a tall, angular women with disproportionately broad shoulders and iron-grey hair.

"Are you Hubert Weaving, by any chance?" she asked in a tone that was unmistakably hostile.

Hubert confirmed that he was, and began his prepared speech. Cheryl cut in straight away and said stonily: "You had better come in for a minute." She led him to a small front sitting room and waved towards a chair, though she did not sit herself.

"What do you want?" she asked coldly.

Hubert forgot about his speech and simply said: "I am really sorry about what has happened, and am here to look at ways the company can help. We will cover the funeral costs, to start with, and we're wondering what else we can do."

"It's a bit late for that, isn't it? My husband was ill, and had been for some time, and he needed help. All you did was destroy him." The tone was cool and measured, but Hubert could sense that there could be a verbal explosion any minute.

"I'm really sorry about—"

"Like hell you are!" said Cheryl Howes. The decibels were starting to increase. "You don't care about people! Only yourself! I have heard a lot about you, and the only reason I said you could come in was for me to see for myself what you're like. I wanted to see if you really were the cold-hearted bastard I had heard about. Now that I know that you are, you can go!"

"But surely—"

"Get the hell out of here!" Cheryl roared. "Get out now!" Hubert could see little point in doing anything else. "That's right, get out... and don't come back!" she added.

And, once Hubert was outside and moving away, he was told: "You said you were sorry. Well, let me tell you this: you are going to be very sorry indeed for what you did. I will make sure of that!"

Hubert beat a hasty retreat and headed for his next port of call. The Bridgetown Drop-in Centre, generally referred to as the Drop-in, was just five minutes' walk away, and he was expected to be there within the next hour.

The Drop-in was in a road reputed to be seedy, and could be found in the middle of a row of boarded-up former shops. The premises had once been occupied by a tobacconist, who had cut his losses and left two years ago. The opening hours were much the same as those for a shop, with the ground floor made available for homeless people to have breakfast, lunch and countless cups of tea or coffee.

Entry was via a front door and a hall with a counter that lay across the hall. The counter was always manned either by a paid member of staff or a volunteer, and their main task was to ensure that no drugs, alcohol or offensive weapons could be taken through.

Hubert was greeted by a sturdy, middle-aged woman wearing jeans and a T-shirt that revealed strong, tattooed arms. The woman made a quick telephone call before opening up one side of the counter and telling Hubert to go up a narrow flight of stairs to the right.

A woman in a trouser suit appeared at the top to greet him. She introduced herself as Violet Lowndes, the director. She shook him firmly by the hand and led him to a spacious but sparsely furnished office shared by two other women and pulled out a wooden chair from a stack of three in a corner for him to sit on.

Violet Lowndes was tall, trim, in her mid-forties and spoke with a cut-glass accent. "I've heard a lot about you," she said as she eyed him speculatively.

"Not all bad, I hope," Hubert responded coolly.

"What can I do for you?" Ms Lowndes then asked.

"It's more a matter of what I... acting on behalf of the *Bridgetown Argus*... can do for *you*," Hubert said, a little irritated that he was not getting the warm reception he had expected.

Ms Lowndes smiled with her mouth, but not her eyes. "We're always in need of support," she said. "Please tell me what you have in mind."

Hubert told her that a fund-raising drive and a sale of some sort had been envisaged.

"The sale could be held here," Ms Lowndes said. "Our volunteers could man some of the stalls, and some of our clients could do this as well. We could also have people standing on street corners with charity boxes."

"That's excellent!" said Hubert. "The next thing we need to do is fix a date."

"Perhaps I could get back to you on that. In the meantime, a feature in your newspaper on the problem of homelessness in Bridgetown would not go amiss."

"I will get my new Editor on to that."

Ms Lowndes then stood up and walked with Hubert to the top of the staircase. "I will be in touch," she said. "We can then start sorting out the details."

Next on Hubert's list of people to see was John Sutherland, the recently elected chairman of Bridgetown Chamber of Commerce. He was known to be a young man in a hurry, and Hubert had good reason to expect him to be on the same wavelength.

"I've heard all sorts about you," he said with a grin after greeting him at his office near the town centre. "You've brought a new broom to the *Argus* and I'm bringing in a new broom for Bridgetown. How can I help you?"

John Sutherland, who owned and ran a chain of shops as well as letting out four of his five houses, listened intently as Hubert outlined his plans for the *Argus* to connect with the public more and, at the same time, involve local businesses. He was much the same age as Hubert, though he was short and stocky in build and paid less attention than Hubert to sartorial elegance.

"Sounds good to me," he said. "I will lay on some support for the Drop-in and have a stall at their sale for starters. I will also place some adverts about my businesses with you. You can call me John, by the way."

"That sounds excellent!" said Hubert. "You won't regret it!"

"I'm sure I won't!" John said impassively. "And, as I say, that's just for starters. If you can keep me informed of any plans you have involving local businesses, I will spread the word. I will, of course, keep you informed of events we know about at our end. That way, we will all be in profit!"

The two both knew that those last few words were a signal for their meeting to end and, after a firm handshake and an agreement to stay in touch, Hubert was back in the street outside. The meeting had lasted for just ten minutes.

The upshot was that he had time to look up the branch manager of an insurance company and perhaps contact a few estate agents before going to the restaurant where he had arranged to dine with Loretta.

The insurance manager was older, quieter, better dressed and more urbane than John Sutherland. He greeted Hubert courteously rather than cordially and, like John Sutherland, said he would be glad to do business with him. "I have heard a lot about you," he said as they parted.

"I still have time to call on some estate agents," Hubert said to himself on leaving.

However, as he made his way to where most of them operated, he passed a café and, on glancing through its plate-glass window, saw two people he did not expect or particularly want to see at that time.

One was Shirley Bell. The other, sitting at a table opposite her, was Sharon, the spiky-haired girl he had met on his first visit to the *Town Bugle*.

CHAPTER 16

"I can see what you see in 'im," said Sharon. "He has a kind of suave but sinister charm that could turn many a girl on." Shirley nodded. "He's not so bad-looking either," Sharon added. "The pointy ears and the Mister Spock looks may not be everyone's cup of tea, but it's a turn-on for plenty."

Shirley took a nervous sip of her coffee before saying: "I have a feeling he's swept quite a few women off their feet."

"Including you?!"

"Yes, including me! I hate to admit it, and I wish it wasn't true. I just can't get over the feeling that, all along, he's just been using me."

Sharon gave Shirley a gentle hand squeeze. "That sounds pretty bad," she said. "If I can be of help in any way, you only need to ask. I will be here for you."

"That's appreciated," said Shirley. "You know, there have recently been times when I have wished that I hadn't left the *Bugle*."

"At the rate things are going, I'll be leaving it, too," Sharon said with a wry smile.

"Oh dear! Is the paper about to fold?"

"It's very much beginning to look that way. It's running out of money fast. Trevor was absolutely livid when he first heard you were leaving. And I don't think I can repeat in here what he said about Hubert Weaving! As you know, he made no attempt to replace you, and he's been scratching around for ways to make money for the *Bugle* ever since."

"No one can accuse Hubert of being Mister Popular, that's for sure!" Shirley observed.

"They certainly can't!" Sharon agreed, with growing vehemence. "I think Trevor, for one, would happily kill him if he had the chance!"

"I gather there are quite a few people at the *Argus* who feel much the same," said Shirley.

Sharon could see that tears were beginning to well up in her former colleague's eyes. "I wonder what the bastard's doing right now," she said.

Shirley began to sob. "He's probably with that Loretta Robey person," she said.

"What, the local glamour model?"

"Yes, that's the one. Hubert has been getting her to take part in some of the paper's promotional activities, which is probably a good idea. The bit I don't like is the amount of time he spends with her, for so-called business reasons. He spends more time with her than with me these days."

"Oh, blimey! I don't like the sound of that!"

"I'm afraid it's true," Shirley added. "In fact, during the last week he seems to have been spending more time avoiding me than actually seeing me!"

Sharon moved her chair close to Shirley's and embraced her. "Just let it all out," she said as Shirley buried her head in a shoulder and wept. "I'm here for you."

Shirley looked up for a moment and asked if there was any point in contacting Trevor about a possible return to the *Bugle*.

Sharon shook her head gravely. "I think we're too far down the road for that," she said. "I could have words with him on your behalf, if you like, but I think it's highly unlikely. There's not the money about."

"What about you?" asked Shirley. "Will you be staying?"

"Good question!" said Sharon. "I suspect possibly not. Trevor has hinted that he might have to let me go before much longer, and I'm starting to look around for something else."

"Are you likely to leave Bridgetown?"

"Not if I can help it."

"I hope that, whatever happens, you stay in Bridgetown," said Shirley. "I really feel the need to have a good friend around just now."

Sharon responded by hugging her more tightly and planting a kiss on her forehead.

As the pair parted and headed for their respective work stations, neither had any inkling of the bombshell that was about to be dropped.

Hubert called in on several estate agency offices, as planned, and, for the most part, was treated cordially. Two or three of the office underlings eyed him with curiosity that bordered on suspicion, but the proprietors and office managers were all glad to see him. They welcomed the fact that, unlike the previous regime, the *Argus* was taking an interest in their affairs and was keen to offer a good service.

"How's Ginger Bell keeping these days?" one of them asked. "I haven't seen her for a bit."

"She's fine," Hubert assured him. "I'm sure she'll be in contact with you soon."

"That's great!" the agent said. "In the meantime, it's good to meet you face to face. We've all heard a lot about you."

The oft-repeated comment was a source of amusement for Hubert, who, by then, had banished from his mind his torrid encounter with Cheryl Howes and was in an upbeat mood by the time he met Loretta.

However, when Loretta arrived at their rendezvous, one look at the expression on her face was enough to wipe away his smile. He asked her what was wrong, but did not need to.

"What are you going to do about it?" Loretta asked anxiously.

Hubert was quick to react. "Don't worry," he said soothingly as he took both her hands into his. "I will do the right thing by you."

CHAPTER 17

Publicity was kept to a minimum after Hubert and Loretta agreed to tie the knot. A registry office wedding was hastily arranged, with the guest list kept to a minimum.

Sebastian was the automatic choice for the role of best man, while a childhood friend of Loretta's acted as bridesmaid. On Hubert's side, the only others to receive invitations were Lord Perryman and Jane Smith. The former declined because of a golfing engagement, while the latter did not receive the news of the engagement kindly and flatly refused to be there.

Loretta's parents had health issues and were not able to attend, and the only other guests of the bride were a cousin and a former boyfriend. Her publicists were kept at bay with the words: "My modelling days are over."

A short wedding report with a picture of the couple signing the register, after the shortest of ceremonies, appeared unobtrusively on an inside page of the *Bridgetown Argus*.

The news of the marriage came as a surprise to just about everyone in the town, though it was, by and large, greeted with indifference. Loretta's modelling career, promoted in the main from early childhood by her mother, was on the wane and only her publicists took more than a passing interest. One of the reasons it was on the wane was that Loretta, who had been pushed into it in the first place, had been seeking a way out. She had grown weary of what she described as 'life in a goldfish bowl' and had, for some time, yearned for a 'normal life' and a 'normal relationship'.

Staff at the *Argus* were totally taken aback, though, once they had digested the fact, the overriding feeling was: "Let's hope the bastard has a long honeymoon!"

The notable exceptions were Jane Smith, who could be heard swearing at the mirror in a ladies' cloakroom, and a distraught Shirley Bell, who ran out of the building and never returned.

The honeymoon was for just a week. Hubert had booked a tiny eighteenth-century cottage that stood alone in a remote part of the Norfolk coast. The cottage lay halfway up a hill and, because it could only be accessed via a narrow, winding path, Hubert had to park his car at the top. The bedroom overlooked the sea, and views of waves lapping over the shore could be enjoyed. When the tide was out, it was possible to walk along miles of sand without seeing a soul.

Hubert and Loretta had known each other for only a matter of weeks, and yet, even before the honeymoon, they really felt they knew each other. It was if mutual understanding and rapport had been put in place as soon as they had first met.

For Loretta, the honeymoon was idyllic. The love-making was all she could have hoped for, and more. The remoteness of where they were, coupled with Hubert's skills as a lover, enabled the couple to act with a degree of abandon that was new to her. She was free!

Until a year or so ago, her life had been in the hands of her ambitious mother. A former beauty queen and model herself, Mrs Robey had wanted Loretta to follow in her footsteps from the moment she was born. When Mr Robey, a one-time Mister Adonis of Bridgetown, died suddenly of a heart attack while their daughter was just starting to attend a local primary school, the mother's ambitions grew. It soon became a case of Mrs Robey living her life through her daughter.

For Loretta, life was like being almost permanently in the limelight. Mrs Robey entered her into every children's beauty contest or fashion event, in any part of the country she could think of, and made sure she was forever clad in the most expensive, figure-hugging clothes possible. There were photographic assignments, too, which enabled Mrs Robey to build up a portfolio on her 'protégée'. There was little time for Loretta to mix with other pupils outside school hours, and there were even times when Loretta was plucked away from lessons so that she could attend some sort of fashion assignment. On such occasions, Mrs Robey was always able to come up with some sort of pretext, and this did much to raise the ire of teachers who did not believe her.

The ire of classmates, who also derided the way she dressed, was raised as well. They believed Loretta was receiving preferential treatment and, as a result, 'Young Miss Bridgetown', as she was often contemptuously referred to, made few friends and was frequently bullied during her schooldays.

Another problem that Loretta had to contend with as she grew older was that she was neither tall enough nor thin enough to cut it in the world of fashion.

A reluctantly reconciled Mrs Robey then resorted to feverishly looking around for ostensibly respectable photographic assignments that her daughter could go to, and kept herself informed of every beauty contest she could compete in.

By the time Loretta left school, she was widely known in Bridgetown as the 'local pin-up'. Her GCSE grades, especially in English, were far better than anyone had expected, though, and Loretta entertained ideas of a career in journalism or even seeking a university place.

Her mother had other ideas, of course. "You can think about that later," she declared. "The life of a glamour model is short and you need to strike while the iron is hot," she declared.

Mrs Robey proceeded to map out Loretta's career by arranging a variety of assignments and ensuring that her daughter kept in shape with a programme of diet and exercise. She took care to ensure that the obviously sleazy photographers were kept at bay, though both mother and daughter conceded that 'topless with taste' was acceptable.

Some of the photographers Loretta encountered propositioned her, and she was not above having the occasional fling. One of these, inevitably perhaps, was with the much older Harry Phillipson, who seduced her after luring her to an empty *Argus* studio. Another affair Loretta had was with a muscular young staff member at the gym where she worked out, and yet another was with the manager of a new supermarket at which Loretta was there to open.

Loretta did her best to keep her mother in the dark about these 'extra-curricular activities', though she strongly suspected that a blind eye was being turned.

In any event, Loretta increasingly felt she was being used in one way or another by just about everyone she came into contact with. No one, it seemed, had any interest in either her welfare or what she was about.

That all changed when Hubert came along. At first, she did not trust him, and she had good reason to believe that he intended to use her, too. She had heard he could be ruthless and, on top if this, she had developed enough nous to recognise a man with his eye on the main chance.

Yet, incredibly, there was a hint of rapport between the pair from the outset. The rapport grew markedly when Hubert began to show an interest in her as a person. At first, it was a matter of asking her about her leisure pursuits and inviting her views on subjects unrelated to the reason they were meeting. Before long, he had her opening up about how she was tiring of modelling, what she really wanted to do with her life and the constraints being imposed upon her.

"If you become a reporter, you will be the first one I like!" Hubert joked.

Loretta was able to laugh, though the sentiment expressed surprised her a little. What mattered, however, was the fact that Hubert really seemed to understand her in a way she had not experienced before. She began to feel that she understood him as well.

She managed to make him open up about himself a little – something she knew few people had ever been able to do – and she even got him to reveal why he had such a hatred of journalists.

The rapport strengthened at such a pace that when they first made love, on a dark and deserted stretch of beach at just past midnight, they gave themselves to each other in a way that neither had done before.

Back in Bridgetown, Hubert took a walk along the same stretch at much the same time of night. He had rented a small but well-appointed flat not far away while waiting for a house purchase to go through. The house was detached, opulent and in the town's most up-market area. Loretta was sleeping heavily and happily, and Hubert's decision to pop out was on the spur of the moment.

The late-night stroll gave him a chance to reflect on his not-so-happy past, as well as how he managed to find love and what the future held.

On a couple of occasions, his thoughts were interrupted by what he thought was the sound of footsteps. However, he could see no sign of anyone being around and he continued his walk along the seafront.

He began to mull over the shake-up he had imposed at the *Argus* and the question of whether it should be intensified or relaxed a little. There were staffing decisions to be made, too, including in particular over how to deal with 'Ginger' Bell… both personally and professionally.

He wondered how much further, if at all, he should go with his cull of those hated journalists. Lord Perryman seemed to love them and clearly had reservations about the actions taken up to now. So there might be a case for Hubert to reign in his hatred for a while.

Perhaps there was even a case for trying to forget the past and the way reporters and photographers had intruded into his personal grief and acted like a pack of hungry jackals. He was, after all, in a euphoric frame of mind, and he decided that now was the time for dark thoughts to be banished.

As Hubert approached the derelict pier, he gave a start as, once more, he thought he heard footsteps but saw nothing. A few moments later, he was startled again when a beam of light was suddenly shone on him. He put a hand to his eyes, and saw the outline of a policeman.

"Are you all right, sir?" the officer asked as he walked towards him, and lowered his torch a little. Hubert was now able to see a sturdy frame and a boy's face.

"Yes, I'm fine, thank you," he said. "I had a rush of blood to the head and decided to take a late-night walk."

"That's unusual, but entirely legal," the young PC said with a quizzical smile. "I don't suppose you have any form of identification with you?"

Hubert was able to produce his driving licence.

"That looks fine, sir," the officer said. "I hope you enjoy the rest of your walk." Now satisfied that he had done his duty, he began to walk away from the seafront and disappeared into the dark.

As it happened, it was his first week of walking on the beat in Bridgetown. He was to learn later that he was the last person but one to see Hubert alive.

CHAPTER 18

News of Hubert's murder became Bridgetown's main talking point the following day. The brutality of the murder sent shockwaves through most of the town, though the mood at the *Argus* could be described by cynics as ambivalent.

The police were alerted in the small hours of the morning, after Loretta woke up from a nightmare and found no husband by her side. The nightmare was about Hubert being hunted in a jungle by hordes of enemies that happened to include Shirley Bell, Jane Smith and two journalists. On awakening abruptly, she had a premonition that something terrible had occurred. She threw on some clothes and instinctively half-walked, half-ran along the beach in the direction of the derelict pier.

The sight of Hubert, battered almost beyond recognition, led to her screaming horribly and running blindly towards the town centre and the police station. Before reaching the station, she caught up with the young PC who had earlier patrolled the seafront and talked to Hubert, and grabbed at him desperately.

Within an hour, an area around the pier was besieged with police officers with torches and dogs. The body was eventually taken away to be examined at a mortuary and the area remained cordoned off during a search for clues.

But there were no clues, just lots of blood. There was no sign of a murder weapon, and any potential footprint had been washed away by the tide. The only fact the police had to go on was that Hubert Weaving had been struck from behind by a blunt instrument and then hit many more times while lying on the ground. Most of the blows had been to the back of the head, the neck and face, though a few had also been directed at the groin area. In all, Hubert had been hit almost a hundred times.

It did not take the police long to realise that there were plenty of potential suspects to be interviewed. After questioning Loretta and expressing condolences, they had words with Hamish McLennan. The fiery Chief Reporter was well known to them, mainly because he handled or oversaw most of the crime stories that appeared in the *Argus*. His temper was known to them, too, and it had come as no surprise to them in the past that he had been in several punch-ups.

"If I find oot who did it, I will give him a wee dram of the hard stuff!" he declared.

The inspector interviewing him knew him well and gave a wry smile. He continued to question Hamish, but could not get him to say anything that came remotely close to incriminating himself.

The investigative team talked to every member of staff, recent past as well as present, at the newspaper, along with the widows of Graham Wormold and Brian Howes, and had words with Sebastian Weaving as well. The officers quicky realised that many of them bore Hubert ill will in abundance, but they could not obtain anything that remotely established proof of guilt of murder. Some of the suspects were interviewed more than once. All were questioned exhaustively.

Meanwhile, word reached the force that a major 'turf war' between drug dealers was imminent. A gang from London had moved in and was trying to oust the main local 'firm', and the Chief Constable declared: "If we don't step in straight away, there will be carnage!" Their subsequent operation was intensive and eventually successful.

The question of who murdered Hubert Weaving was put on the back-burner.

The only certainty was that no one mourned the death of 'The Vulcan' at the *Argus*, not even Jane Smith. There were discussions aplenty about who the killer might be, but of at least equal interest was the matter of what changes were now likely to take place.

Lord Perryman tried to contact Nick Hemsley to tell him that his presence in Bridgetown was needed urgently. He threw down his golf clubs in anger when word reached him on the course that neither the MD nor his aide Claudine Drew had any intention of returning.

There was nothing for it but for Perryman to take the helm himself. His first step was to make Jane Advertising Manager on a trial basis, having heard that Shirley Bell had left in a hurry and since had a nervous breakdown.

"I'm particularly keen for you to keep the estate agents happy," he said to Jane. "We can't afford to lose them again."

"I will do everything in my power to keep them sweet," Jane assured him, as she put away her powder compact and allowed the proprietor to get a glimpse of thigh.

He then had exhaustive talks with Kelvin Ward and Andy McCallum on ways to improve the newspaper's content and, at the same time, bolster staff morale.

"We could do with some really good feature articles," he said at one point. "I'm afraid we are a bit short of writers these days," Kelvin replied, and Lord Perryman hastily went on to the subject of keeping advertisers happy.

Jane's job became easier after a while, when the *Town Bugle* folded due to lack of funds and the estate agents had no one else to advertise with. The *Bugle*'s proprietor had made feverish attempts to secure advertising revenue from other sources, and was said to have been made livid by the influence Hubert had brought to bear.

Life for the *Argus*' journalists became easier, too. The feeling of constantly being under the cosh was no longer there, though Andy McCallum did his best to make them think otherwise, and, in so doing, became the new hate figure.

Lord Perryman, forever a lover of newspapers and journalists, told Kelvin that a new company car and possibly a place on the board awaited him if the newspaper fared well under his leadership. "Nick Hemsley's unexpected departure could mean there will be a vacancy to fill," the Editor was told. Andy McCallum was informed, with slightly less enthusiasm, that 'promotion is not out of the question'.

The rank-and-file journalists gradually became more settled in their roles, though the newly appointed accountant kept a firm grip on expenses claims. The feeling of stability spread to the firm's non-editorial departments, and the influence of 'The Vulcan' subsided. As the weeks rolled by, there was less speculation on who Hubert's killer was and more on who might become the next managing director.

"If Kelvin gets the job, we will at least have someone who knows something about newspapers and running things," one of the reporters observed.

"He'd be an improvement on that tosser Hemsley!" Hamish McLennan agreed.

"One thing's for sure: if the job goes to a journalist, 'The Vulcan' will turn in his grave!" another reporter said.

Hamish chuckled. "The only regret is that I have is that I didn't kill the bastard myself!" he said... not for the first time.

He said much the same while having a drink with Willard Shakespeare, who had got to know quite a few of the *Argus* staff, the next day. The local 'private eye' had also shared drinks with Derek Wormold, Brian Howes, Joseph Finklater and even Kelvin Ward, who had a bitter lemon, on one occasion. He made it his business to get to know the locals, especially those who could be described as 'characters', though he had never got to meet the man who had been murdered.

The question of who killed the 'dreaded Mister Spock' remained unanswered and, although he was highly intrigued, Willard was reconciled to the fact that the matter was of no concern to him.

All that changed on the day Loretta Robey and Sebastian Weaving suddenly turned up at his office.

CHAPTER 19

"Why don;t you start with the police?" said Cicely. "They won't be able to tell you much… but then neither can I!" Willard could sense the tension and was not surprised that his assistant had become tense and tight-lipped.

"I hardly knew Sebastian's older brother," Cicely added. "In fact, I only encountered him twice and then only briefly. He was a good-looking young man, in an unpleasant sort of way, and all I can tell you is what I have told you before: he used to bully Sebastian."

"That could conceivably be a motive for murder," Willard pointed out.

"Yes, I dare say it could," Cicely said testily. "But, if that's the case, why would he come into this office and demand that you find out who the killer was?"

"It seems unlikely," Willard admitted. "But nothing is impossible. It wouldn't be the first time someone had pleaded for a killer to be found when he was the killer all the time."

"What is impossible is for me to tell you who it was," said Cicely. "I can't help you any further with this case… apart from advise you to discuss it with someone at the police station."

Well aware of how increasingly het up Cicely was becoming, Willard decided to discuss the matter no further for the time being. *If I'm not careful, she'll walk out on me!* he thought to himself.

Without further ado, he rose from his desk, put on his jacket and announced that he was 'off to the nick'.

The station sergeant recognised Willard as someone he had seen socially, and quickly arranged for him to talk to an Inspector Richards. The inspector, who had been at the crime scene, told Willard what little he could and wished him the best of luck. "If, by any remote chance, you should come across the murder weapon or anything else that might help us with our enquiries, we would very much like to be told about it," he said.

Willard assured him that if he got lucky, he would tell the police.

The inspector wished him good luck again, before adding with a wink: "There's no shortage of suspects you can talk to, anyway!"

Willard decided his next port of call should be The Tavern, where, with a bit of luck, he would catch up with Hamish McLennan, a font of local knowledge and someone who had to be regarded as a suspect himself. The fiery Chief Reporter had shown himself to be capable of violence, and the fact that he had made it clear what he thought of 'The Vulcan' meant that he could not be ruled out. He would also know a lot about others who had fallen foul of 'The Vulcan' and might well be able to name people he could talk to and perhaps tell him where to find them.

Willard decided to take a stroll along the beach in the direction of The Tavern. As he did so, he caught sight of a familiar figure with a camera in his hands and a parrot sitting on his left shoulder. It was the former *Argus* photographer, Harry Phillipson.

He could see that the 'lothario snapper' had aged somewhat. Harry's hair had grown partially grey and had begun to thin. His once rosy complexion showed signs of greyness, too, and worry lines were now in evidence. He had lost weight and no longer stood totally erect, and he seemed to have lost some of the agility that had once enabled him to take photographs from every conceivable angle.

This was the man who had once been dangled from a helicopter so he could provide footage of a police car chase. On another occasion, he had photographed a fire rescue from a high-rise flat while standing on the steeply sloping roof of a building on the other side of a road. Many a barmaid had drooled over him while he had regaled them with stories of these and other exploits.

"Hi, Willard, long time no see!" he said with a smile, as the latter approached. The smile was still the same, and Willard suspected that the same applied to his libido as well.

Harry suddenly caught sight of a young couple walking nearby and placed his parrot on one of the young man's shoulders and offered to take a photograph. The young man reluctantly agreed and handed over some money, and, once the transaction had been completed, Harry began to talk to Willard again. "How's business?" he asked.

Willard initially held back from saying what he was currently working on, and simply replied that he was 'keeping his head above water' before asking Harry how life was treating him.

Harry's face blackened, and, all of a sudden, he looked five years older. "Pretty dire, to be honest," he replied. "My wife's walked out on me and seems intent in taking me for every penny she can get, and I'm struggling to make ends meet."

"I'm sorry to hear that," said Willard.

Harry, who could sense what was at the back of Willard's mind, then added: "It could be argued that I got my just deserts as far as the wife was concerned. I had, after all, been playing away a bit…. well, more than a bit… and she had had enough. I pleaded with her to give me another chance, but she said she had heard all that before and would have none of it. I don't altogether blame her, really."

"It must be tough losing both your wife and job at the same time, though," Willard then said.

Harry's bright blue eyes flashed ferociously. "Oh, yes! I've got that bastard Weaving to thank for that! I'd love to find out who bumped him off. I could then buy him a drink!"

"The question of who did it remains a mystery, of course."

"Perhaps I should hire you to try to find out!" Harry said, tongue in cheek.

The two men looked at each other for a moment, and it dawned on Harry that someone else had hired Willard to do just that.

Harry wrapped a big hand round a sturdy black torch that he had had lying on a chair beside some of his photographic equipment, and squeezed it hard.

"It might help you to know that, on the night in question, I was in Bournemouth," he said through his teeth. "I had been at a photographic art convention and spent the night at the Seaview Hotel. So you can remove me from your list of suspects… unfortunately!"

As the pair parted, after wishing each other good luck in their respective endeavours, Willard could see Harry's eyes light up at the sudden sight of two shapely middle-aged women in shorts. One of them appeared to give him the 'glad eye', and Harry responded by placing his parrot on one of her shoulders. "Let me make this a day for you to remember," he said to her.

CHAPTER 20

"I can only think of one person who might have benefitted from the arrival of Hubert Weaving," said Hamish McLennan, as he sipped into his latest dram. "That's apart from Jane Smith, the 'fantasy woman', of course." Hamish drew Willard's attention to the fact that his glass had hardly been touched and, by implication, urged him to keep up.

Once again, Willard marvelled at the fact that the Chief Reporter of the *Bridgetown Argus* could remain articulate while under the influence and forever be on the ball when it came to spotting stories or keeping up to date with gossip. He had heard about the 'fantasy woman' from several sources already, but could not fail to express surprise that anyone else, especially a journalist, could prosper under a regime led by 'The Vulcan'.

"I am referring to Mildred Pitt," said Hamish. "As you know, she was an extremely talented feature writer on the *Argus* and yet she still got eased out."

"So, how…?"

Hamish stroked his bushy beard that was once all black but now bore large grey flecks, and grinned. "You obviously haven't read *The Lady on the Pier*?!"

"What, you mean the new bodice-ripper that everyone is talking about?"

"That's the one!" said Hamish. "…and there's a whole series in the pipeline. Mildred has been writing under an assumed name, but, once you've read the blurb on the back about the author, there's no doubt who it is."

Willard expressed amazement that someone as erudite as Mildred Pitt would write a bodice-ripper, especially one as risqué as this one was said to be.

"She's coining it in, by all accounts," Hamish added.

Willard shook his head in disbelief, before saying: "Under the circumstances, it's good to see at least one journalist prospering." Hamish nodded.

"I'd better have a chat with her anyway," Willard added.

Hamish gave him a knowing look. "No doubt you'd like to know where I was on the night of the murder myself!" he said.

"I'm afraid I would," Willard confirmed. "I hope to get in touch with everyone who I know had anything to do with Weaving, and then, if possible, check out their stories."

"Fair enough," said Hamish. "All I can tell you is that I was out on a bender with an old mate of mine… a proper keelie, he was… from the Gorbals. The whole day is a bit of a blur now, but, as far as I can remember, we did not go anywhere near the beach. Paradoxically, I do quite often take a late-night stroll by the sea because it helps to clear my head and gives me a feeling of serenity."

Willard tried to imagine Hamish being serene, before saying: "But not on this particular night."

Hamish then sounded anything but calm, when he added: "One thing I can tell you is that if I had met the bugger on the beach, I would not have used a blunt instrument. I would have given him a bloody good right-hander!"

"I would have hit him with anything I could lay my hands on!" an unfamiliar voice could be heard suddenly from a few feet away.

Willard turned in his seat to see a dark-suited, broad-shouldered man of average height and aged around forty. He had clearly entered the pub a few minutes ago, just bought a pint of bitter and was standing well within earshot. His face looked familiar, but Willard could not immediately place it.

However, as always, Hamish was quickly on the ball. "You're the guy who runs the *Bugle*, aren't you?" he asked.

The newcomer drew up a chair and joined the other two. "My name is Trevor," he said in a distinct Cockney accent. "You've probably seen my face on a *Bugle* poster somewhere. I do own it, but not for much longer... and you can probably guess why."

"That's business, I'm afraid," Hamish said sympathetically. "If it helps at all, I had a consuming hatred of Weaving, too!" The *Argus*' Chief Reporter introduced himself and then Willard, who explained his involvement.

"I suppose you'll have to put me on your list of suspects," said Trevor. "And it's not just a matter of being put out of business in Bridgetown. It's also the way he treated Shirley Bell. She is a lovely lady, and if I had had the chance to get my hands on that—"

"How is Shirley these days?" asked Hamish.

"She's doing her best to put her life together again. You know she had a complete nervous breakdown, don't you?"

Hamish nodded. "I had heard that, but don't know much about the detail," he said.

Trevor began to bristle. "The main *detail* is the way Weaving manipulated her," he said, hardly able to contain his fury. "He seduced her, quite literally, into leaving the *Bugle* and dumped her with total disregard for her feelings once he had no further use for her."

"It sounds, from what you say, that Shirley Bell had feelings for Weaving," Willard volunteered.

Hamish began to bristle, too. "…And all he cared about was getting those fucking adverts back!"

"That's pretty much the size of it," Trevor confirmed. "Incredible as it may seem, Shirley fell for Weaving big time!"

"That *does* seem incredible!" said Willard. "Any idea of how come?"

"She must have been more vulnerable than she let on," Hamish suggested.

"That would appear to be the case," Trevor agreed with a sigh. "She arrived in Bridgetown without knowing anyone in the town, largely to get away from her ex-husband, I believe. She was in no hurry to tell me that, of course. When we first met, I was, after all, just a potential employer. However, I was able to glean that she had been in an abusive relationship and that she wanted to start a new life in a new place."

"It sounds as if you had no qualms about employing her," Willard observed.

"I took her on on the basis that we were both taking a chance," said Trevor. "I own a number of free newspapers in and around London, and my plan was, and still is, to expand into a few seaside towns like Bridgetown. When Shirley visited me, I could see that she was intelligent and articulate and that, although she lacked the relevant experience, she possessed the sort of personality that would win over advertisers... especially estate agents."

"She obviously turned out to be an asset," said Hamish.

"She certainly did. I got her on the cheap, to be honest, and I was all set to bump up her salary when that so-and-so Weaving put his oar in."

"So what is Shirley doing now?" Willard asked. "Is she still in Bridgetown?"

"She is at the moment, though it might not be for much longer. She had a short spell in a mental hospital after her breakdown, in which she took an overdose of something, and is now back in her flat. But I believe her husband is back on the scene, and wants her to take him back."

"Does the husband know about her affair with Weaving?"

"Yes, he's known about him for some time."

"Did he know before Weaving was murdered?"

"Possibly. I'm not sure about that, though what I can tell you is that he was pretty furious when he heard about the way he seduced her and then dumped her."

"So," said Hamish, "that's yet another person who had reason to kill the bugger!"

"And that's one more person I will have to ask where he was on the night of the murder," said Willard.

Trevor gave another sigh, before saying: "Since you're obviously going to ask me where I was on the night as well, I had better tell you."

"OK, now's as good a time as any to get it over with!"

"I was driving from Bridgetown to London," said Trevor. "I had been to see Shirley, to find out how she was and even possibly re-employ her, though that was not the main reason for the visit. I had grown very fond of her, and was even hoping she might have feelings for me."

Willard and Hamish both entertained thoughts of asking whether she did, but were able to stop themselves.

"It became apparent very early on that her heart was for one person only, and that person was certainly not me!" Trevor went on. "I was a good shoulder to cry on, though, and she was able to pour herself out to me a bit."

"What sort of time did you leave her?" Willard asked.

"I can't remember exactly, but it was around 10pm and I was halfway home by the time Hubert Weaving's body was discovered."

"Sorry to ask this, but is there any way you can verify what you said?"

"You could try the attendant at that big car park. He might have seen me, I suppose."

Willard was about to thank Trevor for his help when the latter said: "There is just one more thing... I think I might have encountered Shirley's ex-husband."

"We're all ears!" said Hamish.

"I had just left Shirley's flat and, as I began to walk to where my car was, a big, burly man with sandy hair, a pot belly and the face of a drinker appeared lurching from an opposite direction and said something to me that I couldn't hear."

"Was he aggressive?"

"Yes, he did seem to be. I pretended not to hear him and continued to make my way to the car park. It was not until I was in my car and beginning my journey home that I realised who the man might be."

"Did you check to see if Shirley was all right?" Hamish asked.

"Yes, I stopped at a petrol station phone box and gave her a call. The man fitted the brief description Shirley had given me, and I was worried."

"Was it him?" Willard asked.

"It was. He banged on Shirley's door, and was told to go away and not think about returning until he was sober. Shirley said that it looked for a minute as if he might cut up rough, but, after a minute, he turned round and left."

"Do you know if the husband is still in town?" Willard asked.

"Good question!" said Trevor. "I'm not sure why, but I have a feeling he might be."

"It sounds as if he is yet one more person I am going to need to talk to," said Willard.

"Good luck!" the other two said in unison.

CHAPTER 21

A much-needed piece of light relief was offered the following day. Next on Willard's list of people to see was Eileen Wormold, widow of Derek, the former Deputy Editor. He did not particularly relish the prospect and was well aware that, later on, he would have to talk to Shirley Bell's erratic ex-husband and to the thuggish Sebastian, younger brother of Hubert Weaving. The widow of Brian Howes was unlikely to be a barrel of laughs either, for that matter.

Willard had asked Cicely to check out Harry Phillipson's movements on the day of the murder. His presence at the photographic convention was verified after a couple of telephone calls, and it was quickly established that he had booked a room for the night at the Seaview Hotel.

However, the hotel receptionist told Cicely that Harry did not actually spend the night there. This extra piece of information put Cicely in a quandary for a moment. Fortunately for her, a hotel porter standing nearby overheard the conversation and was able to tell the receptionist that Mr Phillipson had been seen driving off with a shapely young woman who happened to work for a weekly newspaper in Bournemouth.

"I think we can say he's innocent!" Cicely told Willard drily.

Willard was able to laugh, and he was relieved that he could at least eliminate one name on his list of suspects. He was, of course, still reconciled to a situation in which he had to ask a lot of people questions that the police might well have asked already. And there were no real leads to pursue. He had to hope that something unexpected would arise, or that someone would somehow give himself or herself away.

The wreath on the front door of the Wormold household set the tone for Willard's meeting with the widow. Eileen Wormold, who was dressed from head to toe in black, invited Willard to join her in the front sitting room. Having met her before, albeit briefly, Willard was able to see she had lost weight and grown gaunt. The colour in her cheeks had all but gone, and the cool mustiness of the inside of the house matched the mood and suggested that a window had not been opened for months.

Willard, always a keen observer of human nature, summed her up as a woman whose husband had been her whole life. He could guess that Eileen Wormold, as a young woman, had had just one ambition... to get married and have children. As it turned out, there were no children and all her focus had fallen on Derek. She had no brothers or sisters and, once married, there was no room for friends, as she saw her role in life as being devoted solely to Derek. She was there to support him with his work, be at his side socially and share his bed.

"You probably think it is awful of me to say this, but I laughed out loud when I heard Weaving had been murdered," she said. "I was glad he was dead. If it wasn't for him, Derek would still be alive, I'm almost sure of that. He was the world to me, and Weaving took him away from me!" A hint of venom crept into her soft, quiet voice during the last sentence.

Willard gave a sympathetic nod. "I never got to meet Weaving, though I have heard plenty, and he certainly wasn't anyone's Mister Popular!" he said. "I did know your husband, of course, and I have to say that I miss those drinks we had together from time to time."

"I'm not surprised. He was popular."

Willard knew this was not entirely true, as Derek Wormold had a reputation at the *Argus* of letting others do the hard work and receiving the credit for their efforts. He would not have been popular with 'The Vulcan'.

"There are a lot of people who miss him," Willard said diplomatically.

Eileen fished out a handkerchief from a handbag and wiped away a tear. "He was my life," she said.

Willard listened attentively while Eileen told how she first met Derek in a pub, where he chatted her up and dated her. The couple quickly became inseparable, and they were married within a year. Nearly thirty years of bliss followed.

"His passing must have led to a huge gap in your life," said Willard.

"It certainly did. Derek was my everything, and suddenly I had nothing!" The handkerchief came out of the bag again.

"I can see that. Have you been able to do anything, take any steps, to rebuild your life?"

The question made Eileen perk up a bit. "Well, yes, there had been a bit of an improvement during the last couple of months," she replied. "I have struck up a friendship with Cheryl Howes, who goes to the same church as I have been going to lately. I found her a bit scary at first… I can imagine her having a terrible temper… but we do have something in common."

"And I know what that is!" Willard confirmed. "And it's not hard to guess what your favourite topic of conversation is!"

"It was certainly Cheryl's favourite topic!" said Eileen. "She rarely talks about anything else!"

"So… the two of you have a get-together from time to time and talk about bumping off 'The Vulcan'. Have you got anyone else taking part in these discussions?"

"Yes, there's Cicely Harman, a keen church-goer, who often joins us now." Eileen saw Willard's eyebrows rise, and then she twigged. "Oh, of course, she's the Cicely you know, the one who works with you!"

"Good heavens! It's a small world, isn't it? Did Cicely talk about bumping off Weaving as well?"

"Yes, she did! She was none too fond of Weaving either, but for a different reason."

"What was that?"

"Did you know he had a younger brother, called Sebastian?"

"Yes, I have met him once, and I intend to talk to him again."

"Did you know that Hubert Weaving used to bully his brother unmercifully? I heard this from Cicely, who had struck up a friendship with Sebastian. I'm not sure 'friendship' is the right word. They're not the same age and they seem to have nothing in common, but I think that what they have together is a bit more than just a friendship."

"Intriguing!" said Willard. "Can you tell me anything more about the bullying?"

"Only a little bit. When Hubert and Sebastian were boys, the bullying was mainly physical, I gather. As they got older, it became more mental, with Hubert belittling and ridiculing Sebastian at every opportunity and being so domineering that Sebastian could not do anything... not even go out of the house... without Hubert's permission. That's all I can tell you, really. No doubt, Cicely can tell you more."

Willard, who assured Eileen that he would have words with Cicely about this, then asked: "Did Cicely talk about bumping off Weaving as well?"

"Yes, she did a couple of times. As you obviously know by now, Cicely is all prim and proper on the outside. But what goes on inside could, I suspect, be an entirely different matter!"

Willard, who had, indeed, come to a similar conclusion, decided it was time to ask a leading question: "Can you tell me where you were on the night of the murder?"

Eileen Wormold gave a wry smile. "I was at the Howes' household," she said. "We were eating cheese and drinking wine and coffee, and talking into the small hours of the morning. There are no prizes for guessing what we were talking about!"

Before Willard left, Eileen described the fateful incident in which Derek arrived at work, following a period of convalescence from illness, to find his car-parking space had gone. By now, the story had gone round the entire *Argus* building and Willard had heard about it from several sources. He listened patiently and, once she had finished, said: "That's absolutely dreadful!"

"It goes to show the sort of person Hubert Weaving must have been," Eileen added.

"It seems to me that, for some, yet to be explained reason, he had a pathological hatred of all journalists," Willard observed.

CHAPTER 22

Next on Willard's list of people to visit was the formidable Cheryl Howes, widow of Brian, the journalist who committed suicide after being sacked. He did not relish the prospect, as he had met her once and could see immediately she was someone with whom he had to watch his p's and q's.

She lived in a small 'chocolate box' 17th-century cottage with small, impeccably kept gardens and roses round the front door. The front sitting room, the only room that Willard got to see, was in perfect order, too, with not even a hint of clutter. An upright piano occupied most of one wall, and there were photographs featuring Brian everywhere.

"How can I help you?" Cheryl asked frostily, as soon as Willard was seated in the armchair he had been told to sit in.

Willard told her how Loretta Robey and Sebastian Weaving had paid a surprise visit to his office and hired him to find out who the killer was. "I told them that if the police couldn't find out, it was unlikely that I could," he said. "I was reluctant to take the case, to be honest."

The last part of his explanation was far from honest, as he was desperate for business at the time and the case, although seemingly impossible to solve, was the most interesting he had ever been asked to deal with.

Cheryl's dark eyes flashed. "The only thing I can tell you is that the murderer, whoever it was, beat me to it!" she said. "There are quite a few other people who feel the same, including Eileen Wormold, who I believe you have spoken to already."

Willard confirmed that he had seen Eileen, and added: "She has been through a bad time, and I appreciate that you must have as well."

"Did you know that my husband had had mental health issues?" Cheryl then asked. She was now spluttering with rage, and was hard put to get the words out.

"I have heard a little, but not much," Willard replied.

"He had been mentally ill for some time. He had been seeing his doctor, was on medication, and there had been talk of him having a spell in the hospital's psychiatric unit. I had considered having words about this with the Editor, who seemed to be a sympathetic type… though, of course, he isn't around anymore, is he?"

"No, there have been a lot of changes at the *Argus*. Especially at the top."

"Brian was a broken man long before that dreadful Weaving person got onto him. His mind was in such a state that he would have confessed to killing the Editor, if someone asked him!"

"He was clearly a person who needed help."

"That's what he needed, and he needed it badly!" Cheryl said, half-screaming. "If Weaving hadn't come along when he did, he would almost certainly have got it."

"I'm really sorry," said Willard. "I knew your husband slightly, and I liked him. I feel sorry for Eileen Wormold, too, and wish there was something I could do to help."

"I suppose the one way you can help is to find out who the murderer was, and I can then add that person to my list of friends!" The tone was laced with bitterness.

Willard then braced himself before asking the leading question: "Can you tell me where you were on the night of the murder? I'm sorry to be asking this, but this is something I have to ask everybody."

"My answer is the same as the one Eileen has already given you!" Cheryl snapped. "I was with Eileen and your friend Cicely. Cicely has her own reasons for disliking Weaving, and you should be speaking to her about it!"

"You can rest assured that I will. I will be talking to everyone who might, in any way, have been involved, including all the journalists who might have been under the cosh."

"Good! I know a lot of them, and I know all the senior ones, and the only one who seems to have prospered is Mildred Pitt. Hamish has somehow survived, but all the other senior ones have gone under."

"Do you know Joseph Finklater?"

"I certainly do! He is – or perhaps I should say was – a brilliant feature writer, almost on a par with Mildred. Brian used to have literary get-togethers with Joseph, Mildred and sometimes Hamish, and I was always impressed by their talent and intelligence. When they all got together, there seemed to be nothing they couldn't talk about!"

"What's Joseph doing these days? I know him slightly, but haven't seen him for a while."

"You may well ask!" said Cheryl, whose face began to redden. "He's in a drying-out clinic. He's been in and out of it, mostly in, for some time."

"Oh, no! I knew he liked a tipple, but I had no idea it was that bad."

"It wasn't… until you know what! However, he had had trouble with his marriage for years, and his flighty wife walked out on him at around the same time as Weaving arrived on the scene. I'm afraid poor Joseph went to pieces after he was eased out of the *Argus*. He's a lovely man, and what happened to him has upset me almost as much as the death of Brian."

"I will make a point of looking him up," said Willard. "I will need to question him, but it won't be just for that. I will try to see if there's a way I can help him," he promised.

"I will write down the name, address and phone number of the place he's at," said Cheryl, who picked up a large glass paperweight that was holding down a note pad on a small table beside where she was sitting, and jotted down the details.

Willard observed that she had unusually large hands as she passed the piece of paper carrying the details to him. *It's a pity I can't take the paperweight away with me so that I can get police forensics to examine it*, he thought to himself.

That was clutching at straws, of course. His quest to find a piece of evidence, even a tiny piece, that might point him towards the murderer was still ongoing. He still needed to find something that the police were unable to find. He had to hope he could unearth something unusual from someone else, such as Shirley Bell, Lord Perryman, Cicely, even poor old Joseph. He knew, too, that, before long, he would need to give a progress report to Loretta Robey and Sebastian Weaving. Perhaps the glamorous Loretta or the unlovable younger brother could tell him something no one had yet thought of?

His next step, however, was to return to his office to check with Cicely whether there were any messages, items in the post or, if he was lucky, some important piece of information he could get to grips with. He was in no hurry to cross-examine his valued employee, though he knew that, sooner or later, he would have to. His next port of call would be to look up Joseph, after which he would tactfully approach Shirley Bell and track down Lord Perryman.

The ever-efficient Cicely handed over a small bundle of letters, that all turned out to be bills, along with a note of the days and times Lord Perryman could be seen and another note with directions on how to get to Joseph's drying-out clinic. "I'm still trying to fix a time when you can see Mrs Bell," she added.

Almost as soon as she said this, the door to Willard's office was flung open and a burly, red-faced man entered with a lurching gait. Willard knew who he was immediately.

"Can we help you?" Cicely asked in clipped tones that bore a hint of disapproval.

The new arrival ignored the question and, with breath reeking of alcohol, glared at Willard.

"I want you to leave my wife alone," he said. His speech was so slurred that Willard had some difficulty understanding what he was saying.

"I thought you and your wife had separated," he said.

"Well, you thought wrong!" the visitor said. "I want us to give our marriage another go."

Willard, who was not slow to appreciate the delicacy of the situation, wished him the best of luck. "I just need to ask her a few questions in connection with my investigations into the murder of Hubert Weaving. I assure you that I have no wish to upset her and, once I have asked her these questions, should be able to leave her in peace."

The truculent visitor swore and banged a fist on Willard's desk. "Leave my wife alone!" he bellowed. "I won't be telling you again!"

CHAPTER 23

If there was one way dyslexia had helped Willard over the years it was how it had given him the ability to size people up. It had helped him to learn about people generally and, in particular, enabled him to quickly assess whether someone he had never met before was lying or likely to be confrontational. He could see through bluster, and know whether a threat, even if only implied, was likely to be carried out.

His latest visitor was likely to cause problems, especially if under the influence of alcohol. Shirley Bell's husband, assuming he still was her husband, was a big, powerfully built man, who was, in fact, inebriated for much of the time. From what Willard had heard, Shirley Bell had come to Bridgetown to get away from him. And it was not hard to see why.

Willard could see that Mr Bell might well try to hamper his investigations, though there was no way he was going to stop them. The dyslexic sleuth had learned, partly due to force of circumstances, to look after himself. He would avoid trouble if he could, but would deal with it if he had to.

The disadvantages of dyslexia became all too apparent during Willard's childhood. There were hints of his condition even before he started school. His speech development had hardly got off the ground, and he was having extreme difficulties in expressing himself. He was unable to pronounce long words properly and could not remember the right word when trying to put a sentence together. Learning the alphabet was beyond him, as were nursery rhymes and the idea of rhyming in general.

His problems with reading, writing and spelling quickly came to light at his primary school, where most of the teachers recognised that dyslexia did not mean lack of intelligence. Some of his classmates did not understand his condition, however, and Willard had to learn quickly how to deal with derision and bullies. His difficulties included being only able to read and write extremely slowly, confusing the orders of letters or words, and putting letters the wrong way round. He could understand information verbally, but struggled with information that was written down.

On the plus side, Willard was outstanding at problem-solving and he had an almost uncanny ability to 'think outside the box'. These were qualities that were to stand him in increasingly good stead as life went on.

His equable temperament was an advantage, too, and, with outside help, he was quick to realise that he was far from alone in his predicament. He learned that an estimated one in ten people had some form of dyslexia. He was told that the symptoms could vary from person to person and that the severity of the condition varied quite a bit as well. Under these circumstances, and with his outlook on life generally,

Willard chose to focus on the fact that there were others worse off than himself.

Special-needs teachers at school helped him to cope with, if not overcome, many of the problems presented by dyslexia and, as time went on, he became increasingly better at dealing with them.

There were certain situations he dreaded, though, especially during his school days. His handwriting was appalling and he was aware that even the most tolerant teachers could not avoid wincing. His spelling was so unpredictable and inconsistent that it became a source of classroom amusement. His inability to express himself easily was a source of embarrassment, though, with help, he eventually learned to be coherent and even lucid.

Perhaps the greatest problem for Willard was reading, which he could only do slowly, and he would make errors when reading aloud. There were times at school when pupils were required to read aloud passages from books, especially those relating to English literature or history. Willard would dread these times more than any others, as they would often make him the subject of ridicule and cause classmates to assume he was an idiot.

The ridicule would sometimes continue in the playground later on, and could at times lead to bullying. The normally good-humoured Willard… or Willyshake, as he kept being called… was usually able to avoid getting into a fight, but not always. After a while, however, he began to excel in sports, especially contact sports such as boxing and judo, and, by and large, ridicule gave way to respect. He was big for his age, in any case, and the bullies appreciated the wisdom of leaving him alone.

As the years went by, younger pupils increasingly looked up to Willard, who eventually became a house monitor, as well as a role model.

His parents both died at around the time he left the Army, and there followed a period of several years in which he did not know what to do with his life. There was also a failed romance during this period, and Willard was left wondering whether he would ever find someone he could share his uncertain life with.

He had, however, become adept at dealing with many dyslexia-related problems and at getting people to accept him for what he was. No one thought he was stupid anymore!

The main problems that remained were his spelling and his inability to absorb anything that had been written down or printed.

Willard was eternally grateful to the fact that he had found his calling. His abilities at problem-solving and ferreting out facts were being put to the best possible use now.

His reliance on Cicely, who, to him, was far more than a 'super secretary', was heavy, though.

There were certain tasks that were still anathema to him and his reliance on Cicely to relieve him of them was so strong that he was even considering offering her a partnership. A partnership of what, though? At the moment, Cicely was being paid a meagre salary for working part-time... though, if the occasion demanded she would happily work full-time hours for no extra pay.

The last thing Willard wanted to do was risk upsetting her and having her walk out in a state of high dudgeon. His fear of this occurring transcended logic.

Yet he knew that, sooner or later, he would have to question Cicely on where she was on the night that Hubert Weaving was murdered. It was a prospect he feared more than any physical threat, and he was putting off the dreaded day for as long as he could.

CHAPTER 24

"I bear Hubert no ill will," Shirley Bell told Willard. "That might well surprise you. I know he had a lot of enemies, and not without reason, and I am now well aware that he used me." The former *Bridgetown Argus* advertising supremo looked pale and gaunt as she sipped coffee from a battered old mug that was lying on a small kitchen table. "Deep down, I probably always was aware."

"How are you now?" Willard asked. "How is life treating you now?"

"Thank you for asking. At the moment, I guess I'm rebuilding it. My friend Sharon, who I used to work with at the *Bugle*, has been really supportive, and the various therapy and counselling sessions have been helpful, too."

"That's good to hear. I never got to meet Hubert Weaving, though I have, of course, heard plenty. No doubt there are lots of things about him that you know, which other people don't." Willard was genuinely interested in learning more about the subject of his enquiry.

Shirley was quick to see where he was coming from.

"I can tell you one or two things that might well surprise you, but, first of all, let me confirm that I was nowhere near Hubert on the night he met his death. I happened to be in the local mental hospital. It was only for a short period, and I have no wish to talk about it, but all you need to do is contact the place and they will verify it."

Willard nodded sympathetically. He thought of mentioning her husband, but, for the moment at least, decided against it.

"I know, deep down, that he was using me from the first day he began to court me," Shirley continued. "I'm not stupid. Yet, believe it or not, we did have something special between us. There were times he would pour himself out to me and tell me things that only people who are really close tell each other. They were private things, intimate things, that will remain in my memory forever."

"It sounds as if he had a tortured soul!"

"Yes, you could say that! The reason he suddenly deserted me once he had made sure the *Argus* got back the property advertising might be obvious to everyone else, but it was not to me! Hubert and I absolutely definitely had something. I can only think he was so driven by some mysterious trigger in his head that would deny him the chance to have a normal sort of human relationship, and be self-destructive instead."

Willard could not help but be intrigued. Shirley Bell's revelation that Hubert Weaving could have had a soft side might not be of much help in his attempts to find out who killed him, but his curiosity was aroused nonetheless.

"Perhaps he had an unhappy childhood," he suggested.

A hint of a tear appeared in Shirley's eyes. "From what I

have heard, it was terri…" Her voice tailed off with the sound of a doorbell.

The caller turned out to be Sharon. Shirley invited her in and introduced her to Willard.

"So, you're the famous dyslexic private eye who's on the trail of Hubert Weaving's murderer!" Sharon said with a cheeky grin. Her hair was spiky and her voice deep, but the jeans and T-shirt she was wearing suggested to Willard that she was all woman. "I've heard a lot about you!"

"Fame at last!" Willard replied feebly. "I hope what you heard was not all bad!"

"On the contrary," Sharon assured him.

"I think the two of you might have something in common," Shirley then said.

"That's right," said Sharon. "I'm dyslexic, too."

"We must meet up and compare notes sometime," said Willard.

"All for it!" Sharon responded with a wink. A moment later, her face grew grave, as she realised she might have turned up at a bad time and interrupted something important.

"I was just about to tell Mr Shakespeare something about Hubert's childhood," Shirley said after a pause.

"Oh, I'm sorry," said Sharon. "Perhaps it would be best if I left?"

"Don't leave on my account," said Willard, who most definitely did not want her to leave. He looked towards Shirley, who confirmed it was fine for Sharon to stay.

"When you arrived, I was about to divulge some things I have never talked about to anyone before, not even my therapist," said Shirley. "I guess I wasn't ready to before. Well, now I am ready to get it out into the open. And it would help me if I did it in your presence, Sharon."

Sharon walked over to where Shirley was sitting and gave her friend a reassuring hug. "You can say anything in front of me, you know that," she said. "I'm sure you will also get a sympathetic hearing from Mr Shakespeare as well. If he doesn't give you one, I'll thump 'im!"

"I wouldn't dare do anything else!" Willard responded with a smile.

Shirley smiled, too, though she still had to brace herself before speaking. "Hubert had a truly terrible childhood," she said. "He had the most appalling parents imaginable." A pause followed.

"In what way?" Sharon asked.

"His mother was a prostitute who had mental health issues and his father was a pervert... and a swine! They were forever fighting, both verbally and physically, and they were always on the move. They never stayed in any one place for more than a year or two."

"That must have been pretty unsettling for Hubert and his brother," Willard observed.

"They wouldn't have much time to make friends," Sharon added.

"Hubert never made any friends and neither, I gather, did Sebastian."

"Are the parents still alive?" Willard asked.

"No, they both committed suicide a long time ago, at different times. The mother took her own life first, shortly after she and the father separated. They had had the most almighty row, during which the father beat her black and blue... and not for the first time. On this occasion, he managed to break her jaw, and the police were involved."

"Where were the children at the time?" Willard asked.

"They were there. They saw it all, and it was not the first time they had witnessed a beating."

"What happened after that? Did the boys stay with the father?"

"They did at first. The mother moved away on her own, to live with a former schoolfriend, I believe, but soon after that she had a complete breakdown and killed herself by slashing her wrists."

"That's awful. I'm surprised the boys weren't put into care," said Willard.

"I'm surprised the father didn't go to prison," Sharon added vehemently. "That's where he should have been!"

"I have a feeling both those things happened at some point, though I'm not sure," said Shirley. "Hubert did pour himself out once or twice, but I always had the feeling he was holding something back."

"Did Hubert say anything about his father's suicide?" Willard asked.

"Not much. All I know is that it happened a few years later. The boys were with their father at that time, but then, one day, there was a visit by the police and he was taken away."

"Do you know why?" Sharon asked. Shirley shook her head.

"You said earlier on that the father was a pervert," said Willard. "What did you mean by that? Was that anything to do with why the police called?"

Shirley suddenly burst into tears. "I don't know!" she wailed. "All I do know is that he was into child porn and that he was not above indulging in pimping," she said. "The press had a field day, I gather."

Willard was hoping to receive a little more detail, but with Shirley now sobbing uncontrollably and Sharon making gestures to indicate it was time to leave, he rose to his feet, thanked Shirley for her time and made for the front door.

Sharon followed him outside and pressed a piece of paper into his hand before going back in to comfort her friend. "I think we have a few things in common," she said before disappearing.

Written on the paper were six figures, which Willard assumed was a telephone number, and Sharon's name in block capitals and with the 'S' the wrong way round.

CHAPTER 25

"I need cheering up!" Willard told Hamish on the telephone.

"You're not the only one!" the fiery Chief Reporter retorted. "Sounds as if we should be taking a wee dram together!" Just half an hour later, the pair were doing that in their favourite watering hole.

Willard, who was in a far more upbeat mood than he had suggested earlier, told Hamish about his interviews with Shirley Bell and then with Joseph Finklater. "Poor old Joe's in a bad way," he said. "Since he left the *Argus*, his alcohol problem has worsened and he's going to be in that clinic for some time to come."

"That's really sad to hear," said Hamish. "He's been a good mate of mine over the years, and I must make a point of seeing him."

"He'd appreciate that," said Willard. "One good thing about it all… if anything can be called good… is that he can't be regarded as a murder suspect. He was too busy being treated for his alcoholism to be anywhere near where Weaving was bumped off."

Hamish grunted and sighed. "I came close to murdering someone myself last night!" he said.

Willard, who was about to say that, despite his two difficult interviews, he was feeling heartened by the possibility of romance, gave a start. "How come?" he asked.

Hamish described how had had wooed and bedded a new switchboard operator at the newspaper, knowing full well that it was a place where secrets rarely lasted for long.

"We used to go to a remote spot way out in the country, where we were sure no one would see us," he said. "Unfortunately, I had overlooked the fact that working in the *Argus* postroom was a notorious peeping Tom. He's a big fat bloke called Barry. Have you ever come across him?"

"I've heard about him, but never met him."

Hamish went on to describe how he caught Barry watching the pair making love behind a cluster of bushes and handed out a hiding. "He didn't come into work this morning, and I probably hit him harder and more often than I should have done."

Unsure whether to condone or condemn his actions, Willard suggested that, while the *Argus* might not be the ideal place to work, there was no shortage of interesting characters to be found there.

"There's no shortage of changes going on there either," said Hamish. "Kelvin Ward, the Editor, has taken over from Hemsley as MD and Editor in Chief, and a new Editor has been appointed to fill Ward's old job. There is more talk of redundancies, and rumour has it that Jane Smith is to be offered a place on the Board."

"Oh yes! Jane Smith, the *Argus* fantasy woman!"

Hamish gave an ironic chuckle. "She's still a fantasy woman, but she's also a woman to be feared these days!" he said.

"Interesting!" said Willard. "As it happens, I would like to have a few words with her."

"Well, well, that's quite a coincidence! I have heard on the grapevine that she's curious to meet you!"

"Is that something you might be able to arrange?"

"Tell you what," said Hamish. "I have to get back shortly. If you've got nothing else on, you could come with me and see what the whole place looks like these days. You might even get to meet the new Editor."

"What's he like?"

"He seems a bit of a tosser to me! A buffoon! Still, it's early days, and I suppose we should give him the benefit of the doubt for now!"

On arrival at the *Argus* building, Willard noticed that the girls behind the reception desk were younger, prettier and more alluringly dressed than hitherto. He peered through a part-glass door that led to the newsroom, and noticed that the faces were both younger and fewer.

A bearded man with massive shoulders and an even bigger stomach emerged from a door to the other side of the reception area and gave the door to the newsroom an almighty shove. "That's the new Editor," Hamish said. "He used to be a high-up at the *Daily Scandal* in London until he got into a punch-up and had to leave in a hurry. He spent three months working as a salesman for a major furniture chain until this job came up."

Before Willard had time to react, the most nubile of the receptionists called out that Jane Smith was able to see him now and Hamish took him to a lift to the second floor. Jane, who was waiting by the lift doors, greeted Willard warmly and took him to her office. She was wearing a long black dress that both covered and clung to her contours.

"I always wanted to meet a private eye," she said, after pouring out some coffee. "I understand you wanted to talk to me, too."

Willard confirmed that he was keen to meet as many people who had connections with Hubert Weaving as possible. "Apart from helping me get a full picture of what the murder victim was like, there is always the possibility of picking up a bit of useful information, which might not be of obvious value on the face of it, that could lead to the identity of the killer."

"I can't help you with the last bit," Jane said crisply. "I was out of town, staying with friends, on the night of the murder, and this can be easily verified by the many people I was in contact with."

"I hope you won't be offended if I check that out," said Willard.

"Of course not," Jane replied with a smile that came from her lips only. "I will make sure you have all the necessary contact details."

"How did you get on with Mr Weaving personally?" Willard then asked. "What was he like to work with?"

Jane gave him a gaze, and smiled again in the way she had before. "I got on with him fine," she said. "I owe him quite a bit, in fact. He made it clear at the outset what he wanted from me, in terms of work ethic and loyalty, and, when I delivered, he rewarded me handsomely."

"Congratulations!" said Willard. "I hear you have moved up the ladder quite a bit since Hubert Weaving arrived on the scene."

"That's very true. He might not have been everyone's cup

of tea, but he was all right with me!"

"Was he the proprietor's cup of tea?"

"Now there's a question!" Jane said with a wry grin. "He did what he was hired to do, which was to get rid of some of the dead wood and improve the firm's finances, but I have a feeling that Lord Perryman had more than a few misgivings."

"It almost sounds as if Lord Perryman did not really know what he wanted."

"Could be. I think one problem is that Perryman has a love of journalists, while Hubert hated them."

"Why the hatred?"

"I don't know. All I do know is that there was hatred."

"Some bad experience in the past perhaps?"

Jane shrugged her shoulders. "Who knows?" she said. "As it happens, I have an important meeting with the board coming up. Perhaps I will be able to glean something then…"

A moment later, the telephone on Jane's desk rang and Willard took this as a cue to leave.

Once he was back downstairs, he could not resist the temptation of peering into the newsroom once more. Hamish was conspicuous by his absence, and Willard assumed that he had dashed out, as he often did, to tackle an urgent assignment.

The new Editor, whose name he was to learn later was Bill Coombes and who was thirty-three years of age, was too conspicuous for anyone's comfort. One of the young reporters was receiving a tongue-lashing that could be heard throughout the ground floor. The reporter was being told what he had written was too long-winded, and every sentence included at least one expletive.

Once outside, Willard opted to take a short stroll

through a part of the town few people visited these days. The area, which was run-down to say the least, was dominated by grubby cobbled lanes that twisted and turned in sync with assorted buildings that nearly all dated from before Victorian times and were, in the main, dilapidated. He would then report back to base and hand over the contact details provided by Jane Smith to Cicely for his aide to check. The buildings, some commercial, some residential, had been seemingly put up without any pre-planning or rhyme or reason, though there must have been some purpose in the past!

Willard mused over his latest visit to the *Argus* and concluded that here was something else in disarray. He felt sure that what he had seen was not what Lord Perryman wanted.

These thoughts dominated his mind to such an extent that he failed to hear the footsteps of someone who was following him.

As he turned one of the area's sharper corners, something heavy descended onto his head and he fell to the ground. A heavy boot thudded into his side three times and a scuffling sound could then be heard before Willard sank into oblivion.

CHAPTER 26

"You had a lucky escape, by the sound of things," Cicely said in her usual clipped tones, as she looked down on the bed where Willard was lying. "Your attacker, who was under the influence of drink, had gone berserk and he might well have killed you."

"I don't feel very lucky!" Willard retorted. "I'm aching everywhere, and it even hurts to talk. And the doctors won't let me go home yet… Thanks for coming, anyway!"

Cicely pointed out, without really needing to, that he had received blows to the head and was being kept in hospital for a few days as a precaution.

"Perhaps you could give me some idea of what happened," said Willard. "One minute I was walking around Bridgetown's old slum area, and the next I'm lying here."

"Your attacker was Shirley Bell's ex-husband, who for some reason, had it in for you," said Cicely. "Perhaps he thought you were Mrs Bell's lover!" she added ironically. "Anyway, luckily for you, someone came to your rescue."

"Who do I have to thank?"

"There are two people who deserve to be thanked, but I'm only able to mention one of them… and that's Mrs Bell's friend, Sharon. She was the one who phoned for an ambulance and made sure you got here."

Willard tried to sit up, but found the process too painful and gave up trying. "Now you're being really mysterious!" he said with a groan that gave away the soreness. "There must be more you can tell me than that!"

Cicely apologised and told him what she could. "Apparently a young man of yobbish appearance emerged from nowhere while you were lying on the ground being kicked, and came to your aid," she said. "There was a terrific fight. Your rescuer was a lot smaller than your attacker, though, and he was beginning to get the worst of it when Sharon turned up and whacked Mr Bell over the head with her brolly or something."

"God bless Sharon!" Willard murmured. "What happened next?"

"Sharon whacked Bell several times and knocked him unconscious, I believe. The young man involved then ran off, leaving Sharon with the job of contacting the police and ambulance."

"God bless Sharon!" Willard said again.

"God bless her, indeed!" said Cicely. "She will doubtless be paying you a visit soon, if she hasn't done so already. I have a feeling she's taken a shine to you!"

Willard, who was keen to change the subject, then asked Cicely if she knew how the police were dealing with his attacker.

Cicely told him that, first of all, Bell needed to be checked for concussion himself and had, in fact, spent a night in the same hospital, and added that a restraining order was being sought on behalf of his wife. Bell had been in trouble for committing acts of violence in the past and could now face a prison sentence.

Shirley, meanwhile, had left Bridgetown for an address known only by the police and social services.

"You will need to take things quietly for a while," Cicely added. "The interviews with suspects can wait for a while, and that includes the one I know you want to do with me. You can rest assured that, when you are ready, I will help you in any way I can."

A visibly more relaxed Willard nodded gratefully before drifting back to sleep, and Cicely departed.

A couple of hours later, the patient was awake again. Another visitor had arrived, he was told, and his heart soared at the sight of Sharon, who walked up to his bed, leaned forward and kissed him lightly on the forehead.

"Shirley sends her apologies for what happened to you," she said. "She feels responsible, and she hopes it will be possible for her to meet you some time when things have settled down."

"That's all right," Willard replied with a weary smile. "That's fine. More important than that is that I understand I owe you a big thank you for coming to my aid while I was being attacked."

Sharon responded with a beatific smile. "No thanks needed," she said, and Willard could see that her pale blue eyes were dancing. "All you need to do now is let someone look after you!"

"Albert Einstein was dyslexic, and nobody accused *him* of being thick!" Sharon said later.

"Perhaps they did at first," Willard replied, "…and then ended up eating humble pie."

"For the rest of their lives, I hope!"

"Leonardo da Vinci was another one, and he wasn't exactly slow either!"

The pair enjoyed comparing notes on how they had managed to deal with dyslexia during childhood, and were able to wallow in the realisation that so many other people, some of them famous, were in much the same boat. They understood that no two boats were exactly the same, that the degree of severity varied and that the condition manifested itself in different ways with different people.

"Richard Branson's another one," said Willard. "So is Theo Paphitis, another brilliant businessman, and then there's Steven Spielberg, the film-maker."

"Tom Cruise and Keira Knightley are dyslexic, too," said Sharon. "So are Whoopi Goldberg, Jim Carrey and Jamie Oliver. And so was the great John Lennon."

"Not to mention Pablo Picasso and Walt Disney."

"Holly Willoughby's another one."

"Come to think of it, there have been three American presidents believed to have been dyslexic… George Washington, John F Kennedy and George W Bush."

"Wow!" Sharon purred as she snuggled up to Willard. "The best thing of all is that you're out of that infernal hospital!"

She had described a little earlier some of the problems she had encountered as a child. She had found it particularly difficult to express herself, carry out a sequence of directions and learn names, sounds and letters. The resultant teasing and catcalls at school had been merciless.

Life at school gradually became easier following the arrival of a special-needs teacher, who was able to address her problems and, to some extent, minimise them. At the same time Sharon began to excel at sport, earn respect and to tackle tormentors both mentally and physically.

"I can be a toughie at times," Sharon said, as she squeezed Willard's nearest hand and planted a tender kiss on his forehead.

"You are quite a special person, aren't you?" Willard murmured. "I'm certainly not sorry to be out of hospital!"

"I will now make you a special breakfast!" Sharon said matter-of-factly, as she leaped out of bed. "Just relax and leave it to me."

Willard marvelled at her slim, rounded and athletic outline as she moved to a far corner of her bedroom and put on a robe. "How do two meaty kippers grab you?" she asked with a wink.

CHAPTER 27

Willard's ribs were still aching as he entered The Auntie's Tearoom, where he was to give a progress report to Loretta Robey. 'Auntie's', as it was known to locals, was halfway up a sloping cul-de-sac that could only be entered from the road facing the seafront and was about ten minutes' walk from the scene of the murder. Housed in a narrow Victorian semi, it featured a tiny kitchen and two rooms for the customers. The downstairs tearoom offered space for six tables and the upstairs room four.

'Auntie's' was a popular haunt for those who knew of its existence. Among those who did was Cicely, who would sometimes use it as a meeting place for seeing her friends from the church. The friends would often include Eileen Wormold and Cheryl Howes.

Willard winced as he grasped a banister and clambered up a steep staircase. Loretta was there already, sitting by a window, and Sebastian Weaving was with her. They were both wearing T-shirts and jeans, and Sebastian was sporting bruises that more than matched Willard's.

"Mine are better than yours!" Sebastian said with a grin as he pointed towards his marks of battle.

Willard asked Sebastian if he was the one he needed to thank for rescuing him from his attacker, and the latter nodded. Willard shook his hand warmly, and then the latter said ruefully: "I had to be rescued, too…. and by a spikey-haired bird at that!"

"I understand that she's the girl who used to work as an assistant at the *Bugle* and became a great friend of Shirley Bell," Loretta then said.

Willard confirmed that she was and, as he did, looked out of the window and noted that he could see comings and goings from a considerable distance, including along the seafront in either direction.

"She's quite a bird!" Sebastian continued. "I was up against a big bloke and I was getting the worst of it, to be honest. But this bird with spikey hair appeared from nowhere and joined in. She didn't 'arf lay into the nutcase. She whacked 'im with a brolly and gave 'im a right kicking!"

"I understand she was the one who called the police and ambulance afterwards," an amazed Willard said.

"I thinks that's right, though I was a bit woozy at the end!" Sebastian said.

What Sebastian told Willard gave the latter considerable food for thought. The new love of his life was clearly quite a lady! What could be seen from the window was not a fact to be dismissed either!

However, his train of thought was suddenly interrupted by an announcement by Loretta. "I want you to drop the investigation," she said. "I don't want you to be put in any more danger, and you don't seem to be getting anywhere anyway… not that I ever really expected you to."

The temptation to take the money and run was strong. The doctors had told Willard he should rest, and the idea of indulging in any physical activity that was outside Sharon's bed was anathema just now.

Yet giving up was not an option. There was a stubborn streak that saw to that and, in any event, Willard was convinced that, one way or another, he could crack the case. He was not sure how, but he just knew. Perhaps Cicely held the key. But, even if she did not, he felt the truth could be found... and that he could not relax until he found it.

Loretta was astute enough to see what was on his mind. "You don't believe in quitting, do you?" she said before receiving a reply.

"I can't stop now, even if you stop paying me," Willard said.

"Not paying you is out of the question," Loretta said emphatically. "If you're happy to carry on, please do. I just thought it was only right to give you the option."

"We'll look after you!" Sebastian added.

"We also hope you look after yourself, and not think about rushing back to work until you're absolutely sure you are ready," Loretta said.

Willard assured them both he would not overdo things, and be more careful in future.

However, before taking his leave, he raised a question that had been on his mind for some time. "One aspect of this case that has always intrigued me is that Hubert Weaving had such a hatred of journalists," he said. "Do you know if there is any particular reason for this?"

"Most people 'ated 'im!" Sebastian said. His face had reddened, and the words were blurted.

Loretta blushed. "He was a bit of a bully, I'm afraid," she said. Sebastian was shaking, and unable to look anyone in the eye, and, with a gentle hand squeeze, Loretta told him to calm down. "He was all right with me... more than all right... but it was not hard to see that he had a lot of enemies," she added.

"Including journalists?" Willard asked.

"Yes, I'm afraid so," said Loretta, who was beginning to grow nervous herself. "Something happened in the past. I don't know much about it, and I don't want to talk about it. Not now, anyway."

Willard made his way towards his office for a long-overdue talk with Cicely, who, whether he liked it or not, could not be ruled out as a suspect in his investigations. A feeling of slight apprehension was tempered with the thought that his aide might also be able to provide some insight into what made Hubert Weaving tick. He realised, however, that he would probably need to talk to Loretta Robey again, on her own, to have any real chance of satisfying his curiosity about 'The Vulcan''s hatred of journalists.

The walk entailed passing a pub called The Earl of Bridgetown, and he considered popping in for a quick half first. Hamish McLennan appeared in the doorway and helped him make up his mind.

"I'm considering quitting the *Argus*," Hamish announced as soon as the pair had sat down with two whiskies at a corner table. "The whole place has gone bonkers. The paper's going to pot, everyone feels they're under the cosh and the situation has got so bad that there's talk of Lord Perryman selling and walking away while he's still ahead."

"How come it's got so bad? Is the new Editor the problem?"

"He's certainly part of the problem!" Hamish said with a snort. "Apart from being a foul-mouthed bully, who's forever talking about the possibility of redundancies, Bill Coombes says he wants the paper filled with tits and bums and nothing in it that he calls arty-farty!"

"What about Kelvin Ward, the new MD? What does he have to say about that?"

"We don't see much of him. He appears now and then to challenge expenses claims, and we believe he is behind the recent decision to do away with much of the local feature writing and replace it with material bought in from agencies. A lot of the stuff that appears in the *Argus* these days can be seen in other newspapers throughout the country."

"So what does Ward do when he's not in the office?"

"That's a good question! What I can tell you is that if there's any kind of junket in the town, at which a press presence is requested, he'll be the one who will go."

Willard voiced sympathy, and said he could easily see why Hamish wanted to get out. He was not surprised either that Lord Perryman was thinking on the same lines. "I would like to meet him," he added.

"No problem!" said Hamish, who suggested he popped into the *Argus* building tomorrow. "I understand he will be there all morning," he said. "He's been popping in quite a bit lately, though I must warn you that he's not quite the urbane composed character he used to be. He's been like a cat on hot bricks lately, and is clearly not a happy man!"

CHAPTER 28

"He was a vicous bully!" Cicely said with a degree of vehemence that Willard did not think was possible. "He made his younger brother's life a misery!" Willard realised more than ever that he needed to be circumspect with his questioning, though he was also well aware that, apart from Loretta Robey, no one had a good word to say about Hubert Weaving.

"What did he get up to?" he asked.

Cicely took a deep breath before describing how Hubert insulted, ridiculed, slapped and punched Sebastian, who was two years younger and considerably smaller, on an almost daily basis during their childhood and even adolescence. He would get other children to pick on him, too, and play a succession of nasty tricks, such as locking him up in a wardrobe and leaving him there for hours.

"Didn't the parents know what was going on?" Willard asked.

"His father did. He was a bully himself and when he was around, which was not always, he would knock the boys about. He would often beat them with a belt and, when he wasn't doing that, he would encourage the older brother to beat the younger one up."

"What about the mother?"

"From what I have been able to gather, she could be violent, too, though, for much of the time, she was in and out of mental hospitals."

"That sounds terrible! Did the two boys have to fend for themselves a lot of the time?"

"Yes, they did. Another problem was that the family never stayed in any one place for more than a year or two. So Social Services did not know what was going on, and the neighbours often had no idea. By the time anyone was alerted to the fact that all was not well, they were in a different part of the country."

Cicely, who pointed out that Sebastian had always found it difficult to express himself, said she gathered that the two brothers had both spent spells in care and that they had been subjected to other forms of abuse. The abuse did not take place in the care homes.

"The person responsible for that was the father," she added, as she opened her handbag and fished out a tissue. "He died in prison, and I hope he's rotting in Hell!"

Cicely went on to say that the father, Hughroy Weaving, met the mother-to-be, Marylin Mason, at a strip club in Bristol. The latter, a part-time prostitute with severe mental health issues, was with child at the time. She had no idea who the biological father was, and, when, after a few weeks, Hughroy invited her to move in with him, she did so readily. "They got married and Hubert was born soon afterwards."

A year or so later, they moved to Leicester, where Hughroy apparently had a couple of dubious business associates.

He took no interest at all in Hubert's upbringing, and instead forced his wife to go back into prostitution in order to help fill the Weaving coffers. A year after that, Sebastian was born, and about six months after that they moved to Plymouth to get away from creditors. "It would appear that Weaving Senior was involved in all sorts of nefarious activities that included drug trafficking as well as pimping."

Further moves followed, to Oxford, Cambridge, Newcastle and York, and the moves were interspersed with periods in care for the boys. One such spell occurred while Hughroy Weaving was in jail for drug-dealing.

As the years went by, Marylin aged a great deal and her use to Hughroy as a prostitute diminished. At this point, Hughroy began to associate with paedophiles who had an interest in young boys.

"I can't tell you much about that because Sebastian refuses to talk about it," Cicely added. "What I can tell you is that the mother committed suicide and the father died in prison not long after."

"Where were the family when that happened?"

"I don't know. It became quite a scandal at the time, and the press took more than a passing interest."

"I should imagine the two boys were severely traumatised by all this," said Willard. "In fact, I would be amazed if they weren't!"

Cicely confirmed that this was certainly the case with Sebastian, whom she had met through the church, and that she desperately wanted to help him.

"I don't give a damn about Hubert," she said. "He was as big a bastard as his father, and I'm not in the least bit surprised that someone wanted to kill him."

"You must have been harbouring such thoughts yourself!" said Willard.

A long pause followed, during which Cicely gave Willard a knowing look that caused him to fidget.

"And now we come to the sixty-four-dollar question!" Cicely said at length. "You want to know what I was doing on the night of the murder and what, if any, my motives were. I'm right, aren't I? I can see you have been nervous about asking me, and I think I can see why."

"I thought you might take offence and walk out on me," Willard admitted.

Cicely smiled and, as she did, the lines on her face that lent themselves to an aura of prim severity disappeared. "You have no need to worry on that score," she said softly. "I love working here and I will gladly tell you anything you need to know."

A visibly relieved Willard said he would be grateful for any information she could give.

"All right, let's start with motive," said Cicely. "I had that all right. What you may not know is that I met Hubert Weaving a couple of times, and, even though the meetings were brief, I could see what he was like. You never did meet him, did you?"

Willard admitted he had never had the dubious pleasure.

"I could see straight away that he was a bully, who took a delight in making other people's lives a misery," Cicely said. "This particularly applied to poor Sebastian, who he bullied mercilessly."

"Even in your presence?"

"Perhaps especially in my presence. The rudeness and ridicule were constant, and Hubert even manhandled Sebastian in front of me once."

"Was he unpleasant towards you?"

"Oh my goodness, yes! We were both subjected to innuendo and lurid remarks about our relationship. He called me an ageing cradle-snatcher and worse, and was crude in the extreme. I can honestly say he was the most unpleasant person I have ever met."

"I'm truly sorry," said Willard. "It must have been awful for you. It's not hard to see that you both could have had a motive for murder!"

"There was more than a motive. There was intent!" Cicely said vehemently. "I was one of a group of three people who were plotting to kill the bastard! But we didn't do it... unfortunately!"

Willard almost jumped out of his chair. "Who were the others, for Heaven's sake?!" he asked. "Was Sebastian one of them?"

"No, not Sebastian, bless his heart! He may look like a thug and act like one at times, but I know he would not have it in his heart to commit an act of such extreme violence. No, the others were Eileen Wormold and Cheryl Howes. They had even more reason to bear a grudge than either Sebastian or yours truly."

Cicely described how the three would meet and talk about the way Hubert Weaving had affected people's lives. Eileen and Cheryl would pour themselves out about what it was like to be widowed and how Weaving's actions had affected their husbands when they had been alive, their relationships and inevitably their children and other members of their families.

Cicely had been able to pour herself out about her relationship with Sebastian, their age difference and her desire to help him and be there for him.

At first, all the three women wanted to do was talk. However, as they continued to vent their anger together and unite in their hatred of Hubert Weaving, their thoughts gradually turned to murder.

"We used to hold meetings on the top floor of 'Auntie's', the place where you met Loretta Robey, and talk about how we would do it," said Cicely. "We would take it in turns to follow Hubert Weaving's movements, and noted that he would often like to take a late-night walk near the derelict pier. Our idea was to lie in wait and get him in the way that someone else actually did. We were beaten to it!"

Willard could see that Cicely was shaking, and he thanked her for being so open with him. However, there was one question he had to ask: "Are you absolutely sure that person couldn't be Sebastian?"

Cicely began to blush. "No, as I have already said, he does not have it in him to commit murder... In any case, on the night in question he happened to be with me."

CHAPTER 29

"Ouch!" said Willard. "It's still a bit tender just there."

Sharon apologised. "It looks as if I'll have to be gentle with you for a bit longer!" she added.

"Not much longer, I hope!" Willard replied. "I feel a lot better than I did yesterday. It's just that one area on one side that feels a bit naughty. Anyway, I have people to see. Where's my breakfast?!"

Sharon patted his rump. "You must be getting better," she said. "You're getting quite cheeky!"

Willard got up, threw on some clothes and went to the kitchen. "I'm a past master at boiling eggs," he called back. "Do you fancy one?"

Sharon replied that she did. "It's about time you did some of the pampering!" she quipped.

"Do you fancy coming with me?" Willard asked half an hour later.

"No, thanks," said Sharon. "I've had my fill of the newspaper business for now, even if it's a chance at getting a glimpse of the former competition. The *Argus* isn't what it used to be, in any case, and all the interesting characters that were there once seem to have gone."

"Hamish McLennan's still there... though not much longer, by the look of things. He's thinking of getting out."

Sharon, who then said she had some housework and shopping to do, conceded that Hamish *was* a character. "Perhaps you could send him my best wishes," she said. "I have met him in the past, and he seemed all right... even if he is a bit fiery!"

A feeling of peace with the world and utter contentment consumed Willard's mindset as he walked towards the *Bridgetown Argus* building for his meeting with Hamish and then with the newspaper's proprietor.

He did not know who murdered Hubert Weaving or why the victim had such a hatred of journalists, but he was convinced that it was just a matter of time before he found the answers to both questions. And there was no doubt in his mind that, having tried his hand at other jobs and been unfulfilled, he was now in the right vocation, even though he had fallen into it almost by accident.

And, to cap it all, he had fallen in love, in unexpected circumstances. It seemed as if fate had presented him with the prefect partner and soulmate.

"Hello, you got out of the right side of bed this morning, didn't you?!" a grinning Hamish said as he greeted him at the *Argus'* front entrance.

"I don't know what you mean!" Willard replied dreamily.

"Of course you don't, and I don't know who was on the other side of your bed!" Hamish retorted with a wink. A smiling Willard shrugged his shoulders.

After explaining at the reception desk the purpose of his visit, Willard could not resist the temptation of walking to the door that led to the newsroom and peering through the glass to see what was going on in there. He was able to observe the menacing figure of the man he knew to be Andy McCallum, the Deputy Editor, pacing slowly along lines of desks and stopping intermittently to look over someone's shoulder. On a couple of occasions, he leant over a shoulder, snatched a piece of paper from a desk, glared at it for a moment and then plonked it back to where it was.

"He doesn't do that when I'm around," said Hamish, who suddenly loomed up behind Willard. As Willard waited for Hamish to expand on his statement, a receptionist called out to say that Lord Perryman was ready to see him.

Willard could hear the sound of golf club on ball as he knocked on the boardroom door. After being invited to enter, he could see that the owner of the *Bridgetown Argus* was practising his putting in an area at the end which had been earmarked for such a purpose.

"Do take a seat," Lord Perryman said as he pointed towards a large, well-polished desk that had six chairs located nearby, picked up three golf balls that were lying close to each other and carried the balls and putter towards where he then sat. A collection of clubs in a bag and another bag containing cleaning materials sat nearby.

"It's just a matter of time," he said, as soon as Willard was seated. "I've had enough of the newspaper business, and it's just a matter of time before I sell up and get out. I used to love the business, but it's not the same any more. The *Argus* is going to pot, as you can doubtless see. It doesn't have the same people on it anymore, and they're not producing the sort of newspaper I want, the sort of newspaper I can be proud of… and I've had enough! The golf course beckons!"

Willard could see that Lord Perryman's face bore worry lines that were not discernible in the various photographs he had seen of the proprietor. He looked ten years older, his eyes were both weary and restless, and the cool, aristocratic bearing for which he was renowned no longer existed.

"Is there a potential buyer?" Willard asked.

Lord Perryman removed a golf club from the bag it was in and began to polish it feverishly. Most of the metal was gleaming already, but his focus was on one small area which seemed to bear a stain that was either real or imagined.

"One of the troubles with golf is that the grass can discolour the clubs, especially if there's dew about," he said. "No, there's no buyer yet, though I'm sure it's just a matter of time."

Willard then asked what he thought of Hubert Weaving.

The proprietor sighed volubly and put the golf club and polish onto the floor beside where he sat. "Yes, of course, that's why we're here, isn't it?!" he said. "Appointing him might have been the biggest mistake of my life. I've certainly never taken on someone I disliked so much before!"

"You must have had good reason at the time," Willard suggested.

"Point taken! The newspaper was in deep financial trouble, there were disciplinary problems and something had to be done. The only answer seemed to be a new broom, and that unfortunately came in the obnoxious form of Weaving!"

"I never got to meet him, but I've heard plenty and to say he was not popular is clearly a massive understatement!"

"And that brings us to why we are here," Lord Perryman said again. "You want to know where I was on the night Weaving was murdered, don't you?"

Willard nodded.

"I was out and about," Lord Perryman said, as he picked up the golf club he had been polishing and polished it some more. "I was in Bridgetown attending meetings some of the time, but I was also in Seaborn a couple of miles down the road and in London, too. I was all over the place! I have no recollection of being near the pier where the dirty deed took place, but you'll have to take my word for that. There's no one around who can either prove or disprove what I have just told you."

Willard realised there was nothing for it but to thank Lord Perryman for finding the time to see him and to ask for contact details in case he needed to get in touch again.

"Do you play golf, by any chance?" the latter asked as the two men rose to their feet and shook hands. Before waiting for an answer, the *Bridgetown Argus'* proprietor took a club and a ball to the makeshift putting area and smote the ball so hard that it left a dent in the opposite wall.

Willard went downstairs to re-join Hamish, only to learn that the Chief Reporter had had to go out urgently on a job. This was by no means an unusual occurrence, largely because the mercurial Hamish was opting to be away from the office more and more as time went on. An unconcerned Willard knew he could catch up with him later.

However, before leaving the building, Willard felt compelled to have another peek through the door to the newsroom. He could see that, on this occasion, it was the new Editor Ben Coombes who was making his presence felt.

He was red in the face, gesticulating wildly and bellowing at one of the reporters. The reporter was an erudite-looking newcomer.

"Don't you understand?!" he roared. I don't want to see any more grey, arty-farty rubbish in the paper! What we need are lots of tits and bums!"

CHAPTER 30

Could the murder weapon have been a golf club? Willard asked himself as he walked back to his office. *Why was Lord Perryman polishing his clubs, and one spot on one club in particular, so feverishly?* And, *Why was the proprietor of the* Bridgetown Argus *acting in such an erratic and frenetic manner?*

Willard turned over these questions in his mind over and over again. The main reason he did so was the way Lord Perryman had behaved. He was a man known to give an initial impression of being an aristocrat with not much on top – in the mould of the P. G. Wodehouse character, Bertie Wooster – when, in fact, this was far from the truth. Equally well known was his calm, confident and unflappable demeanour. What Willard had seen was a man acting totally out of character.

Willard decided that the first thing he should do was consult Cicely, whose orderly mind and common sense he valued. He would then talk to the police, see if they would consider re-opening the case and perhaps seek out someone with a knowledge of forensics who could make an assessment.

One of the key questions was motive. Lord Perryman had made his dislike of Hubert Weaving abundantly clear. But how could dislike, even intense dislike, on its own be seen as a cause to kill?

As he approached his office, he could see that Loretta Robey was waiting for him. She was standing in the street about twenty yards away from his workplace, and greeted Willard with a wave. "I need to talk to you in private," she said.

"Tell you what, let's meet upstairs at Auntie's in, say, half an hour," said Willard.

That gave Willard just enough time to pop in, say hello to Cicely and ask whether there were any important messages. He was keen to talk to Cicely about his meeting with 'a very edgy Lord Perryman', but reluctantly accepted that such a discussion would have to wait.

Loretta was sitting by the same window as the one Cicely said she used to sit near during her get-togethers with Eileen Wormold and Cheryl Howes. She was dressed dowdily and conservatively, and was clearly in no hurry to be seen in public.

"There are some things I need to get off my chest," she said as soon as Willard had sat. "There are things I really need to talk to someone about, and that someone might as well be you."

"Are these things to do with Hubert Weaving?"

Loretta nodded. "I am well aware that Hubert was not liked and that he had a lot of enemies," she said. "But there are things that hardly anyone knows about and, if they did know, they might not be so quick to condemn him."

Loretta went on to describe Hubert's childhood and how his parents were, and Willard said he had heard about these problems already.

"But do you know why Hubert had such a hatred of journalists?" she asked.

Willard had to admit that he did not, and so Loretta went on to describe how reporters hounded and pried on the whole family at times when Hubert and Sebastian desperately needed help.

"Wherever the family moved, there would, sooner or later, be reporters and photographers hanging around the front door," she said. "Cameras would be flashing and anyone moving in or out of the house could expect to be bombarded with questions. There were even occasions when some of the journalists somehow managed to get inside, and it was the Devil's own job getting them out again!"

The two boys would even be pestered with unwanted questions on their way to or from school. "It didn't seem to matter where the family moved to. The journalists would, sooner or later, find out about them… and, once more, the whiff of scandal would fill the air!"

Inevitably, the boys would be ostracised, teased and bullied at every school they went to. The words 'pimp' and 'paedo' would be used at every opportunity.

Loretta paused for a moment while she opened her handbag and took out a tissue.

"That's all I'm able to tell you really," she added. "I don't doubt that there's more, probably a lot more, but that's as much as I know."

"I wouldn't be surprised if you were the only person Hubert Weaving could confide in," said Willard, who was sensing that here was a young woman with an exceptional ability to understand people and who had been misunderstood frequently herself.

"I'm almost certain that is so," said Loretta. "There was so much he had bottled up in him, and I think that at least some of it had to come out. I don't suppose anyone, not even poor Sebastian, who doesn't always understand what's going on, will know everything that happened. There will be newspaper cuttings, of course, but they won't say it all either."

"There is one thing that's clear to me now," said Willard. "It's not hard to see why Hubert had such a dislike of journalists!"

Loretta gave a tearful laugh. "I'm glad I've had the chance to have a good talk with you on your own," she said. "I might not have helped much with your investigations, but you have been a good listener and that's much appreciated."

Willard was about to explain how being dyslexic had, in a way, helped him to become better at assessing people and at listening to them, when a sudden commotion could be heard outside.

It soon became apparent that a violent scuffle was taking place. Willard looked out of the window to see a familiar figure using a golf club to batter the prostrate form of a large man. He knew he had to act quickly.

Willard dashed downstairs and ran towards where the trouble was taking place. His suspicion that the man with the golf club was Lord Perryman was confirmed. The man on the ground looked familiar, too, though he did not recognise him immediately.

Lord Perryman, his face contorted with rage, was hitting the man on the ground again and again. "I did not go into newspapers for the benefit of bastards like you!" he screamed. His eyes were bloodshot and it seemed as if the last vestige of sanity had deserted him. "You're killing my favourite newspaper, and now I'm going to kill you!"

Willard reached him as he was holding the golf club high and was about to bring it down on the man's head with all his might. He snatched the club from his hand and, as he did, he could see that the victim was Ben Coombes, current Editor of the *Argus*.

Lord Perryman's first reaction to the intervention was to throw a wild punch, which Willard was able to avoid. The second was to sink to the ground, sit with his head in his hands and to weep uncontrollably. Ben Coombes lay motionless, and it was hard to tell whether he was dead or alive.

At this point, Loretta appeared by Willard's side and informed him that the police and an ambulance were on their way.

CHAPTER 31

Champagne corks were popping in Willard's office a few days later. It was a time for celebrations all round. Loretta had re-kindled an old romance, Hamish had secured an attractive retirement package and Willard and Sharon had agreed to form a partnership in more senses than one.

"The detective agency could be re-named 'The Dyslexic Duo!' a smiling Cicely suggested. "Don't you agree?" she then asked Sebastian, as she gave him a maternal look and a pat on a thigh. Willard grinned.

"It's good to be at this gathering, but I'll be gone in less than a week," said Hamish. The new management at the *Bridgetown Argus* had offered him the sort of deal he had been holding out for, and now he was all set to join a younger cousin and help him run fish farm about twenty miles from Oban.

"I will be gone, too," said Loretta, who, purely by chance, had met an old flame while taking a short break in Portugal. "My parents did not approve of him because they thought he was common and did everything they could to break it up," she said. "Now they're not around and I can make my own decisions. He's a fitness coach, and I will be helping him run a gym in Finchley, in London."

"Good luck to you," said Sharon. "I hope it works out!"

"Perhaps we can visit your gym in between cases," Willard suggested.

Loretta responded by congratulating him, not for the first time, on managing to crack the latest one. "What's the latest on Lord Perryman?" she then asked.

"I've heard that he might plead insanity, or whatever we're allowed to call it these days," Willard replied. "It had been established that the wounds inflicted on Ben Coombes were the same as those received by Hubert Weaving, and, during the course of his ravings, Perryman has as good as admitted to killing Weaving."

"And he came close to killing that so-and-so Coombes as well," interjected Hamish.

"Why did 'e do it?" Sebastian asked.

Hamish suggested that Lord Perryman's obsession with running successful and influential newspapers had become so strong that he could not bear the thought of the *Argus* going downhill any more.

Willard agreed that this was as good an explanation as any. "Lord Perryman and Hubert Weaving had a bizarre association, to say the least," he added. "One of them had a love of journalists, while the other hated them!"

"I don't blame my brother for 'ating 'em!" Sebastian said vehemently. "'E 'ad good reason to!" Cicely smiled at him maternally and squeezed his nearest hand.

"One thing we do know is that life in Bridgetown is never going to be the same again," opined Sharon.

"That's certainly going to apply to its newspaper," Hamish said.

Rumours had been abounding that the *Argus* was about to be taken over, and Hamish now confirmed that the giant Jackson's Press had moved in. Jackson's, a conglomerate with a head office in Billericay, Essex, owned more than thirty provincial newspapers throughout the country, and was constantly on the lookout for new acquisitions.

The *Argus* building was to be sold off, and staff were to move to the building that once housed the *Bugle*. There would be just one edition a day, instead of three, meaning fewer staff were needed. The press agency that had been supplying much of the material lately was to be replaced by another agency, which was already providing content that could be used in all the Jackson publications.

Ben Coombes, who was convalescing from his attack by Lord Perryman, had been offered a redundancy package and was to be replaced by the Deputy Editor of a Jackson newspaper in Norfolk. Andy McCallum, a name already known at Jackson's, had resigned, and it was understood by everyone that anyone leaving the *Argus* was unlikely to be replaced in the foreseeable future.

However, thought had been given to bringing back Shirley Bell. Whether she would have been tempted was open to conjecture as no one had been able to find her.

The role of Jane Smith, meanwhile, was under review, the general opinion being that she had her value as a 'meet and greet' person.

The position of Kelvin Ward remained undecided as well. The idea of having a journalist on the board had its appeal with other journalists, and a Human Resources Manager was being sent in from Billericay to monitor the performances of Ward and others.

"I'd love to know what Lord Perryman thinks about all these changes, assuming he knows about them," said Sharon.

"I remember that there used to be lots of wonderful feature writers on the paper," said Loretta. "What has happened to all those wonderful features?"

"You can kiss them all goodbye!" said Hamish. "What you're going to see in future is a minimum of local news and lots of advertising supplements. The rest of the content will all be sorted at head office."

"I'm beginning to feel sorry for Lord Perryman," said Cicely. "His great mission in life was to produce brilliant newspapers and what's going on now must be agony for him!"

"The only good thing I can see is that there will, hopefully, be no more bullying," said Hamish. "There had been a bit of a bullying culture creeping in while Weaving was at the *Argus* and, with a bit of luck, that will come to an end. The top brass at Jackson's are known to be anti-bullying, so things could improve in one respect."

"I should imagine that's something the Human Resources man will be keeping an eye on," said Cicely.

"Thank goodness there's a bit of hope somewhere!" said Willard. "Perhaps we should be talking about something more cheerful. We are supposed to be celebrating, after all!"

"Point taken!" said Hamish, who then asked, with a wink: "When are you and Sharon going to tie the knot?"

"Don't be so cheeky!" a grinning Sharon said. "You'll know when we know."

"It won't be long, and when we have a date you might even get an invite!" Willard added.

"'Ow about a toast?!" Sebastian suddenly suggested. "To the bride and groom!"

"Why not?" said Cicely, who patted him on a leg once more. "To the bride and groom!"

"I suppose we'd all better stand up!" said Loretta. "You might as well do the proposal, Sebastian."

Willard and Sharon began to grow a little red as Sebastian began to say: "'Ere's to the 'appy couple—"

However, he was interrupted by the opening of a door and the massive frame of Aubrey Forsdyke filling the space. "Oh dear, I'm so sorry if I'm interrupting something," he said as he looked around him. It was his turn to look embarrassed.

"That's perfectly all right!" said Willard, who was far from sorry about the interruption. "Is there something I can do to help you?"

Hamish took this as a cue to leave, and he immediately led almost everyone out. Even Cicely made a bee-line for the exit.

"Don't worry about Sharon here," Willard said to the new arrival while pointing towards his fiancée. "She's working here now, and anything you say to me can be said to her as well."

Aubrey Forsdyke began to grow crimson. "I'm having trouble with Estelle again," he said with an air of desperation.

"Are you worried again that she has been seeing another man?" Willard asked.

"No," Aubrey replied. "She's been accusing me of have an affair with another woman. I started to go to a keep fit class recently, and Estelle thinks I have fallen for the woman who runs it. Please believe me that it's not true. She's twenty years older than me, she has a moustache and is reputed to be only interested in other women. I need you to help me clear my name!"

This book is printed on paper from sustainable sources managed under the Forest Stewardship Council (FSC) scheme.

It has been printed in the UK to reduce transportation miles and their impact upon the environment.

For every new title that Matador publishes, we plant a tree to offset CO_2, partnering with the More Trees scheme.

For more about how Matador offsets its environmental impact, see www.troubador.co.uk/about/